# A Heart of Stone

This Large Print Book carries the
Seal of  Approval of N.A.V.H.

# A Heart of Stone

## *Renate Dorrestein*

**Translated from the Dutch by
Hester Velmans**

**Thorndike Press • Thorndike, Maine**

Originally published in Dutch under the title *Een Hart van Steen* by Uitgeverij Contact, Amsterdam. English translation published in Great Britain by Doubleday, a division of Transworld Publishers.

Published in 2001 by arrangement with
Viking Penguin, a division of Penguin Putnam Inc.

Thorndike Press Large Print Basic Series.

The tree indicium is a trademark of Thorndike Press.

The text of this Large Print edition is unabridged.
Other aspects of the book may vary from the original edition.

Set in 16 pt. Plantin by Minnie B. Raven.

Printed in the United States on permanent paper.

**Library of Congress Cataloging-in-Publication Data**

Dorrestein, Renate.
    [Hart van steen. English]
    A heart of stone / Renate Dorrestein ; translated from the Dutch by Hester Velmans.
      p.  (large print)  cm.
    ISBN 0-7862-3229-3 (lg. print : hc : alk. paper)
  I. Velmans, Hester.
  PT5881.14.O67 H3413 2001
   839.3′1364—dc21                 00-054461

For Hilde

# *Contents*

## *PART ONE*

## *PART TWO*

*Part One*

# Frits — college years, autumn 1956 or 1957

There were already four of us by the time Ida arrived, on an unusually cold summer's night. Thanks to a nearly full moon, it was still so bright out at two a.m. that we could count the freckles on each other's noses. We had vowed not to go to sleep until we'd heard the new baby's first cry. We had taken chips and Cokes up to our attic bedroom and had put on our warmest flannel pajamas.

I had made myself a comfy nest on Kester's bed with a stack of pillows. To kill time, he and I were reading a *Batman* comic book together. He would give me a soft poke in the ribs when it was time to turn the page. Our sister Billie, at her usual post in front of the mirror by the clothes closet, was engrossed in snipping off the split ends of her long black hair with nail scissors. And Carlos was on his feet in his crib crooning with excitement, groggy with sleep, his tummy bulging over his drooping diaper. We called him Carlos because as a baby he'd been the spitting image of that gawky English Prince Charles.

It was getting toward the end of the summer holidays — I remember it vividly. Every night you'd discover fat leathery ticks between your toes which, if you believed Billie, had to be twisted out counterclockwise, or you'd get Rocky Mountain spotted fever. We had been out picking blueberries that day; our teeth were still blue. Kester was the only one who had brushed his. Of late, my brother had become embroiled in a grim struggle with the world's dirt. He scrubbed his armpits daily, his face too, but he still smelled, and he always managed to look like some smudged old scrap of newspaper. To show him it didn't bother me, I'd loll against him every now and then as we were reading.

He was sitting cross-legged on his red bedspread, his feet pulled up under him. His toes had recently begun sprouting stubby black hairs, which embarrassed him no end. Having lost interest in the outcome of the Batman story, he picked up Billie's nail file from the floor and began digging under his nails with it.

Our beds were pushed against the four walls: we each had our own domain. Sometimes, if we were having a fight, we'd draw lines on the floorboards with chalk to mark off our territory, or we would conceal rank, slimy finds that we'd fished out of the pond under each other's sheets.

"Is it going to take much longer, do you think?" wondered Billie, sitting down next to me.

Kester drew the file backward with his thumb, then shot it, humming, in her direction. "Shouldn't we be boiling water or something?"

"It's not the High Chaparral here," said my sister, scratching at her calf, bored.

We sat slumped together for a while, too tired to think of any good new distractions. Finally Kes offered in English, *"You don't have to love me, Scarlett. Just kiss me."*

Billie cried out, *"Oh, Rhett! Darling! Don't get killed!"* She toppled over backward, wringing her hands and moaning. Then she bounced upright again, saying, "Wait, now I have one for you."

*"Casablanca,"* I explained to Carlos, who was rattling the bars of his crib.

Billie and Kes started laughing, God knows why. Billie's long hair rippled over her shoulder like a pennant, and I could smell Kester's socks. And for some reason my heart suddenly gave a little lurch, like an old clock pendulum that has to be nudged into ticking again. What a miserable summer it had been. It had all started with Carlos's accident — no, it had started before, on Easter Sunday, after the egg hunt, when my father abruptly announced there would be a new addition to the family. He kept taking his glasses off and then putting them on again, one of his little quirks when he couldn't come up with the right words, and peered at each one of us in turn with a shy, triumphant look. I had this feeling that we should shake his hand and congratulate him or something.

We were all sitting around the kitchen table, about to dive into our Easter breakfast. My mother said, "You children may come up with a name."

"Ramona!" I blurted out. It was a song by the Blue Diamonds, *Ramona! Ramona! Oo-hooh!*

"What if it's a boy?" asked Kester.

Startled, I pushed a twist of hair into my mouth and began to chew on it: didn't he like the idea of another sister?

Billie said indignantly, "There's no room in the attic. If there's another one, I want my own room."

"Oh, darling," said my mother absently.

"I'm fifteen!" yelled Billie, as if that explained it.

We all looked at her in surprise.

"I need a little *privacy!*"

"A little what?" asked Kester.

Later I asked my mother what Billie had meant. "I don't know exactly, Ellen," she said. "That you're all growing up, I suppose."

In my diary I noted, fuming, that I did not care for "such vague answers." I was fond of foreign expressions like "privacy," which was why I couldn't stand it that Billie, who was only at the local high school, had employed a new word before I'd had a chance to acquaint the family with it. When the holidays were over I would be entering a fancy prep school. I'd be translating Livy and Homer. "Was the ancient world familiar with the concept of 'privacy,' " I wrote in my diary, "or is that a modern-day notion?"

I usually got an A for my essays; I suspected the reason was that my teacher probably had to consult a dictionary in order to follow my train of thought. Actually, my cleverness was often a little much to take, even for myself. "Are we what we think?" I wrote in my diary, and, in all honesty, I hoped the answer was no.

★ ★ ★

We were all proud of our house, with its yellowed-newsprint smell and its filing cabinets stacked up to the ceiling. It was a lovely old-fashioned house back then, before that horror of a renovation, with steps out front and a tiled hallway and a basement kitchen. Seeing it sitting there always made you feel happy and safe as you pedaled home along the quiet oak-lined lane that curved languidly up to the old riding stable. In winter we'd race our sleds down the middle of the street, that's how little traffic there was. To think that was only twenty-five years ago!

Practically the entire house was taken up by the archives, so there was no question of clearing out one of the rooms for Billie: what on earth would we have done with all those files? The only space that had never been swallowed up by my parents' clippings service was the cellar beneath the kitchen, because of the damp.

After a heavy downpour, water would seep through the cellar walls, collecting in dismal puddles that flickered with oily patches of yellow and blue. This did not deter Billie, however. She began moving in the very next day, on the Monday after Easter. She laid a grid of platforms and

16

gangplanks over the cracked cement floor, using wood she found in nearby dumpsters — old doors and wormy shelves. You could see the water glistening underneath. She hung up burlap to hide the mildewed walls. She burned incense to mask the musty air, and there were candles smoldering in every corner.

We were allowed to come and visit her new abode just once, and then we could get lost.

Kester said she'd catch gout in that stalagmite grotto and then she'd grow twisted as a corkscrew. Out of spite he built himself a treehouse in the walnut tree behind the house. On its rickety door there hung a large sign: "NO ENTRY TO UNAUTHORIZED PERSONS." Every time I read those lopsided letters, I could hear his new, breaking voice squeaking in my head, the voice that had been giving him as much trouble as the hair on his toes.

Billie and Kes adamantly shut themselves up in their bastions for the duration of the Easter holidays, and so there was no one to show my report card to, with its six A-minuses and two A's, and the rubber stamp of a little raccoon wearing a hat. I couldn't figure those two out at all. I pictured Billie sitting at the bottom of the

17

slippery cellar stairs: her face both sullen and indifferent, her skin pale from lack of daylight, her hair all matted from the humidity. What on earth was she doing down there? Was she practicing to be a mermaid? And Kes, in his tree, was he studying to become an orangutan?

I started brooding about the little creature in my mother's belly who was responsible for all this, and impulsively told my father that they should call her Ida, because it was the ugliest name I could think of. Ida rhymed with spider, and if you twisted the letters around and added a few more, you got diarrhea. How she'd be tormented, later, at school! Serve her right.

Every night, before bedtime, I'd prepare two plates of sandwiches. One I set down by the cellar door, the other I'd take outside. I can still feel the grass wet with dew beneath my bare feet and hear the garden's cryptic silence under the stars. Sometimes there would be the startling hoot of an owl, a noise that for some reason always brought me close to tears. It seemed to me that the nighttime universe was just too vast, too infinite for Kes, who had such a hard time with math. He was just hopeless when it came to numbers. The worst thing was, I couldn't think of a way of letting him know that his existence was important, important to me anyway, out there in his treehouse. What I did in the end was pry open my bicycle bell and pull out all the little cogs; I left it in a rusty little heap in the grass where he couldn't miss it. Kes never knew what to do with himself if he didn't have something to keep his hands busy. Give him two nuts and a bolt, though, and he was in his element. He might not be the world's greatest genius when it came to the times tables, but when you saw those fingers of his at work, you just had to admit you had an extraordinarily talented brother. He could also play a tune on the musical saw. Which is more than most people can say for themselves.

For Billie I always tucked in one of my father's Lucky Strikes next to her sandwich.

Then I'd take a few big gulps from the bottle of gin in the hall cupboard. That way I'd be sure to pass out as soon as I got to bed and wouldn't have to think about the fact that it was only Carlos and me now, up there in the attic. Carlos was nearly three and never got tired of asking questions. "*Why* are the cows in the meadow?" "*Why* is the grass green?" With every *why*, his eyes would bulge at how big

19

and mystifying the world was.

To me, those two weeks were what the world generally was to Carlos: a confusing, hostile muddle. I did not understand then that all things do pass in the end, and that, funnily enough, they usually do so without any help. And that is exactly what happened this time. One fine morning, Billie simply showed up again at breakfast, in a skintight sleeveless ribbed turtleneck, without offering us any explanation for her subterranean sojourn. Nor did Kes mention his own treehouse exile when he too suddenly reappeared at dinner, worn out and smelly. I was sure their return to the house had something to do with my twelfth birthday the next week — a celebration neither of them would dream of missing, of course.

The morning of my birthday I was so excited that I woke up at the crack of dawn. From his crib, Carlos was whimpering his first *why* of the day. The curtain wasn't drawn all the way, and a shaft of dusty light fell on his blond curls, which made him look more like a cherub than ever, if a miserable one.

"Why what?" I whispered.

"Why isn't it *my* birthday?"

"Because it's mine." I had asked for a

dog. Billie was going to teach me to smoke; she had been promising me all year. From now on I was going to start making a fuss over my hair; you were supposed to spend hours making your hairdo look as casual as possible, if you didn't want to be a loser. I'd start having pimples on my chin and crabby moods. Everyone would say, "That Ellen is getting to be such a big girl."

I was also sure that starting today I would no longer get that sour feeling in my stomach at the thought that Billie was the oldest, Kes the firstborn son, Carlos the youngest, and I was the only one who didn't have a special position in our family, which meant that nobody would miss me if I suddenly disappeared. "But the third child is the best child," my father used to console me. "The third child is the cement."

Every time I was down in the dumps, I would write in my diary about being the cement, but I'd have preferred it if my father had just pulled me onto his lap, with my cheek against the scratchy tweed of his jacket, so that I could listen to the thumping of his heart, the contented heartbeat that said, I am your father and I like you just the way you are.

He had turned twelve himself, once. So

he ought to understand how important this day was to me. Only Dad was the kind of man who didn't ever say very much, even though, like some other mild-mannered people, he could totally lose it at times, and lash out at you out of the blue.

I couldn't stay in bed a minute longer. In the back pocket of my jeans there was a long list of dog names I'd been working on since Christmas. Some were underlined in red. As soon as I saw my dog, I would know which of them was his name.

After getting Carlos dressed and taking him downstairs, I saw that the door to the pantry was closed. I listened intently for any sound of clumsy puppy paws scrabbling on the tiles. To give myself something else to think about, I quickly set the table, taking the blue plates from the kitchen cupboard. Mother had designated those as our party dishes. When it was nobody's birthday, we used the white ones.

Just as I was finishing, Kes came into the kitchen, a monster zit on his cheek. He didn't look at me but softly whistled "Happy Birthday" as he stood buttering a slice of bread.

Nearly choking with excitement, I filled the kettle at the tap and put the water on to boil.

"Maybe we'll go to the movies this afternoon," my brother ventured after several minutes, his mouth full.

I gave a yelp of delight.

"Me too!" shrieked Carlos.

I grabbed a cracker and began smearing it with butter. "No way, silly piggy, it's *my* birthday."

"I say," said Billie, from the doorway. She was wearing a long white Indian-cotton dress, with red embroidery around the neck that had little mirrors worked into it. Sometimes she was so beautiful that you just couldn't believe someone as good-looking as that could be your sister. I knew she had been making out with boys at the swimming pool every summer since the age of thirteen, and that she currently had two boyfriends: one had a motorbike, the other his own room. They weren't supposed to find out about each other, and this had already netted me Billie's entire collection of makeup samples.

She glared at me severely. "You haven't by any chance peeked in the pantry, have you, Ellen?"

I shook my head no. My heart was pounding in my throat; my longing pierced my rib cage like a lance.

"Shut your eyes," said my big sister.

With my hand on the pantry handle, I squeezed my eyelids so tight that I saw white sparks.

"So, young people," came my father's voice out of the blue.

I opened my eyes, and there were my parents standing in front of me, their hair uncombed, the sleep not yet rubbed out of their eyes.

"It's my birthday," I said breathlessly.

My mother was smiling as she came toward me. Her robe hung open over her pink nightgown. Underneath you could see her stomach, which already stuck out a bit. When she bent down to kiss me on the top of my head, I got a whiff of her special smell, an indefinable odor that I used to find vaguely disturbing. It wasn't until four years later, when I lost my virginity to Jasper Staalman in the bicycle shed of the Rainbow, that I was finally able to place it: it was the tepid scent of sex that used to hover about my mother every morning.

"Good God," she said, abruptly standing up straight, both hands clutching her belly, "I feel the baby! For the first time! Here, give me your hand, Ellen, feel. Isn't that a wonderful birthday present?"

"Me too!" yelled Carlos. He jumped up, arms stretched out.

"Watch out!" I screamed.

But in his wild rush Carlos had already knocked into the stove where the kettle was whistling up a storm. It capsized. Boiling water gushed over my little brother and poured, steaming, down his neck and chest. He opened his mouth wide in pain and disbelief; he gasped for air, and he roared.

Billie pushed my mother aside and flung herself on top of him.

"Sybille!" my father cried. "Under the cold shower with him. Hurry!"

We all ran after them, Kes and I ahead of the others. Carlos's screams echoed through the stairway. At the top of the landing, through the open bathroom door, we could see Billie crouching next to him under the shower. She was trying to hold the thrashing little body under the ice-cold jet; the red embroidery on her dress was beginning to run and her bra-strap showed through the wet cotton.

"Charlie!" I cried. "Know what? You can come with us to the movies this afternoon, OK?"

Billie looked up. Her wet hair was plastered all over her face. In a muffled voice, she was saying something inconceivable. She was saying, "Sorry, Ellen. I'm so sorry."

I shoved my hand into Kester's palm. I had bitten my tongue: my mouth was flooded with the coppery taste of blood.

"Call the ambulance, Kes," Billie said calmly.

"His neck is coming off," my brother stammered.

"Shhh. It's only his skin."

On the landing we bumped into our parents. My mother was asking something in a worried voice, still clutching her belly. Under that stretched skin of hers lay Ida. Lay Ida plotting even more mischief.

Without bothering to answer my mother, Kes and I stormed down the stairs. The muscles in my fingers still ached days later, that was how tightly I was hanging on to his wrist. We had to toss a ton of clippings off the little hall stand to find the phone, but somehow the ambulance did get there, complete with its team of spirited paramedics. They stuck needles into my little brother, slung slippery bags of fluids over sharp hooks, and rushed him to the hospital. And from that moment on, it was as if Carlos had never existed.

The thought that he might die was so unbearable that I couldn't stand to think about him. So I just canceled him out altogether; I scrapped him from my memory banks, him and that little voice of his always asking questions, and that grubby teddy bear he used to suck on so noisily in bed. The ambulance hadn't even turned the corner before I had forgotten all about my little brother. Everything was right as rain with me. I was the only one who didn't walk around with red-rimmed eyes. My only problem was that I couldn't for the life of me figure out what to call my dog. Instead of the endearing little puppy I had anticipated, for whom I had composed my list of forty-six promising names, he turned out to be a great big black brute from the pound. A secondhand dog. Seeing that he must have noticed my disappointment, I had quite a job reassuring him. "You're fine just the way you are, really you are," I swore. He wagged his tail glumly.

Since there was no way I could fall asleep anymore, not even after chugging down twelve gulps of gin, I'd often go out to the garden at night with Dog. We got into the habit of lying facedown in a hollow under Kester's treehouse. There we would lie side by side, motionless, listening to the lupines sprouting, the earthworms and the slugs grubbing. We could hear moles burrowing and the loathsome

27

bishop's weed sending out new, furtive roots into the flower beds my mother had planted with larkspur and columbine. Underneath us, some sort of colossal peristalsis was at work, an unstoppable force driven by nothing but the need for survival. The fact that life went on was a given, but that didn't mean you had to expect it to make any sense or expect it to be fair.

Next to me, Dog sighed. His breath smelled of old raincoats, and, out of contrition, I vowed I would make him happy. I pressed my cheek against his velvety nose. After all, he had no one but me in the world.

Lack of sleep made me giddy, but more than that, it imbued all my good intentions with a certain feverishness. Every night I would come up with some new resolution, something big and momentous, like the one about Dog, though in the light of day I never managed to carry out any of my objectives. Every day I disappointed myself all over again — I couldn't even keep my stick-insects alive by remembering to supply them with fresh ivy leaves. I kept finding them lying dead in their glass tank, and then I'd quickly cover their eggs with warm sawdust.

★ ★ ★

When the time finally came for Carlos to come home, I had no nails left to bite and my lips were chewed to shreds. It was June, the hydrangeas were in bloom, cream cakes had been ordered, but I was not happy. The fact that my little brother was still alive only meant that I could lose him all over again, a thousand times over, in a thousand diabolical ways. All things considered, it was better not to have a little brother at all.

When I made these thoughts known, Kes said I was well on my way to becoming a Buddhist. Billie thought I was just being a negative creep and twisted my arm behind my back to make me repent. Then she let me try on her new nail polish: "Miss Helen," a lurid pink, in a little potbellied bottle she'd stolen from the drugstore. Carlos was supposed to come home sometime midmorning. Mama and Dad had gone in a taxi to fetch him. Billie prepared a pitcher of juice made from greengage plums and set it, together with six glasses, on the table in the garden. Skin transplants, she informed us, pulling up one of my socks and tucking Kes's shirttail into his pants, took time to heal. Seeing Carlos might give us a shock, but we mustn't let it show.

29

The weather was odd, oppressively warm and yet windy. It got to be noon, and a couple of drowned wasps were already bobbing in the pitcher among the melting ice cubes when Kes suggested, "Do you think they could have had an accident?"

Billie said if he didn't shut up she'd flip her lid; I went to the far end of the yard and plonked myself down on an upside-down bucket. Oh man, I kept saying to myself, oh man. That usually helped. Oh man: you could pretend to be Trini Lopez or John Wayne. Their faces were familiar to us from the clippings, and nothing ever seemed to bother them, ever. I liked Richard Burton; Sean Connery too, I *really* dug him. Kes and I would interview each other in English with an empty toilet paper tube. *"So, Sean, did you like being double-oh-seven?"*

*"No, actually, Ellen,"* Kes would answer, poker-faced, *"to be quite honest with you, I hated every minute of it."* That would set us off; we'd be doubled up with laughter, literally doubled over, the way I was now from lack of sleep.

At two o'clock a taxi stopped in front of our house.

Our parents had taken Carlos into town for ice cream and they had bought him two boxes of Legos. The sun made them squint as they clambered out of the car, Dad carrying Carlos in his arms, followed by Mama and her fat belly — as if they were emerging from a different, more intimate reality and now had to reconcile themselves to the fact of our existence, a fact which seemed to take them by surprise, to put it mildly.

Dad carried Carlos to the largest wicker armchair on the terrace and carefully lowered him into it. Our brother was smothered in bandages from his chin to his waist, which made his shirt bulge all the way around.

"Hey, Quasimodo," said Kester. Then turned crimson.

I was such a bundle of nerves that I burst out laughing. Dog started to bark, loud and shrill, as if to make me behave.

"Welcome home, sweetie-pie," said Billie. She rushed up to him in her bell-bottoms, which she'd made herself from an old pair of Levi's that she had ripped open along the seams to insert triangles of fabric printed with forget-me-nots. She hunkered down beside him and grasped his naked little knees, which looked so pale and defenseless. They should have been sunburned and covered in dirty scabs. Oh man. Without warning I was suddenly *that* close to tears. A little boy of three with spotless knees, didn't that just blow your mind?

"Billie," asked Carlos, squinting against the light, "why is the sun shining?" He sounded listless and no longer glared at you furiously with that helpless urge to understand the world. His big blue eyes were still in the same place, as were his mouth and his nose, and even the little dimple in his chin was still there, unscarred, but he didn't look like Carlos anymore. He looked like Clint Eastwood, the way Clint Eastwood might have looked if he had spent the whole winter at the North Pole with all the cows from *Rawhide*, clubbing baby seals to death to survive. Oil and blubber, that's what you needed against the cold.

"The sun is shining so it can show you its happy face," chanted Billie, "so that little boys —"

"Wrong, you idiot," I yelled, incensed. "The sun shines because the earth turns, because everything turns, all the planets, and the stars too, and the moon, and the Milky Way, and God!" Suddenly I saw it all before me, plain as daylight: all that spinning and careering up there in outer space — it was a wild scene, that was why every once in a while something or other was bound to topple over and crash. They might swear to you that your brother was still alive, but you could see perfectly well with your very own eyes that the old Carlos was dead.

"Ellen," said my mother, "try not to spoil the atmosphere, will you?"

I was speechless with fury. It was that mongrel Ida that had brought this disaster on Carlos, not me. *In ancient Greece, families were permitted by law to leave their unwanted offspring on the garbage heap. In Sparta, babies that did not pass muster were sometimes flung off cliffs or carried up to Mount Taygetus.* That's what it said in the dog-eared ancient-history tome that my father and I had picked up at the second-hand book sale held in my prospective school's auditorium. We'd felt so out of place there that we'd both been sweating like pigs. I had clung to his hand as tightly as I could.

"Would you like a yummy éclair, Michael?" asked my mother.

"Carlos," I said loudly. "His name is Carlos."

"Ellen!" my father warned.

I was so enraged by now that my head was throbbing. The idiots should never have named my brother Michael Adrian. If your name didn't fit you, you didn't stand a chance. Fate wouldn't know where to find you if you needed protection: it was like being on the wrong list; it led to the most dreadful accidents.

That was when Carlos looked up at me. I got goosebumps all over as we gazed at each other for the first time. I wanted to say, Carlos, you're fine just the way you are, I mean it, really. But that would have been a lie. So I turned and wretchedly started passing around the éclairs.

Even now, twenty-five years later, whenever I see a news show about burn victims, or sometimes just like that, for no good reason, I'll ask myself if it ever got better, that lurid, shiny skin on his throat, his chest, and his left arm. It seemed much too tight for him; just looking at it made you feel you were choking. But he must have had quite a bit of plastic surgery over the years. I probably wouldn't even recognize him now if I met him in the street. The last time I saw him, he was five, at his new parents' house. He was young enough to start a whole new life. I was fourteen; nobody wants to adopt you when you're that old.

In those days there was the Matla clippings service in The Hague, and Vaz Dias, and later Euroclip. We were known simply as Van Bemmel, but we were the only ones specializing in Americana. As a small business, you were better off finding a distinct niche for yourself in the marketplace.

Every morning when we set off for school, the student interns who did the clipping for us would arrive on their bicycles; at the same time the couriers dropped off their daily stacks of newspapers and magazines. Officially the business took up the two middle floors of our house, where in six rooms the snipping took place at long tables, according to subject: culture, politics, sports, show business, crime, science and technology. The gray metal filing cabinets, however, took up every available inch of space in the house, including the sunroom. You'd find clippings in the most unlikely places, where someone had dropped them for a moment because the phone was ringing or because someone was at the door. You weren't supposed to touch; it was an iron rule, because if you moved those clippings, no one would ever be able to find them again.

When I had nothing better to do, I liked

to sit on the stairs between the first and second floors; from that perch, if all the doors were open, I could see into all the rooms. The backs of my knees tingled with pleasure at the sight of my parents maintaining seemingly effortless order over the manifest chaos of Bureau Van Bemmel, simply by sitting at their desks. To show my appreciation, I'd sometimes smear my lips with a red M&M. You had to spit on it until the color came off. Once, when I was about ten, the soggy candy accidentally slipped through my fingers and landed on a pile of clippings on the step below me. When I leaned over to pick it up, I saw that it had landed smack in the middle of Henry Kissinger's wide forehead.

We had Kissinger a good thousand times over; we were up to our eyeballs in Kissinger; we had as much Kissinger as we had war vets on the steps of the White House. Impulsively, I grabbed the cutting, folded it in half, and sat on it.

I just sat there after my wicked transgression, rooted to the spot. It was as if I could hear, from all six rooms of Bureau Van Bemmel, the accusing snap of scissors and the rustling of newspaper pages being turned suspiciously. There was a smell of freshly brewed coffee. Somewhere a door slammed. I could hear the whinnying laugh of Marie-Louise, the theology student who had been clipping the showbiz news for us for years. Finally my heart rate returned to normal. I thought of the first-rate job I did for my mother drying the dishes every night: by the time I was finished I was always drenched to the skin because of the way I cradled each dish carefully to my bosom. What was *one* Kissinger, in light of that?

At that thought, I leaned over and lifted the entire pile of clippings onto my lap. I should be able to get away with just about anything. I was about to prove it too. The paper was soft and a little greasy. It was easily torn into long strips. The strips I shredded into little snippets.

I suddenly pictured my father, seated at his desk, or my mother, poring over the card index, abruptly wondering: Goodness, where have the last six months of Kissinger gone? My reckless mood immediately turned to horror. In mounting panic I stared at my hands, which kept on tearing and ripping of their own accord. I burst into tears, but I couldn't make myself stop. It was just like that sinister fairy tale about the girl with the red shoes, whose feet wouldn't stop dancing, not even when her own mother was at death's door.

Somewhere in the universe, Kissinger was at that very moment stepping off a plane to initiate peace negotiations, and before anyone even had a chance to say *"Hello, mister,"* his face, with its optimistic smile below the crimped hair, would disintegrate into hundreds of tiny little scraps.

*Tell us, Henry, didn't you hate being torn up?*

*No, actually, Ellen, I enjoyed every minute of it.*

My father was going to be furious. He would shake me, I would see little flecks of foam collect in the corners of his mouth, and we would both realize that I was more than just cement.

To make sure I wouldn't escape the punishment I so richly deserved, I openly displayed the shredded clippings by strewing them on the floor of our rabbit Moos's hutch, but I was never found out. My parents attributed the missing Kissinger file to the fact that Esmée, our politics clipper at the time, happened to be out of commission for a while with mononucleosis. "The kissing disease," they said, chuckling and shaking their heads.

Every clipping was dated by the students and labeled by category before landing on

my father's desk — a never-ending ava-
lanche of shootings, society weddings,
moon-walks, Oscar ceremonies, race riots,
rodeos, political scandals, beauty pageants,
and armed robberies.

My father sorted everything according to
subject. He made up the files; that was his
job. When journalists called looking for information on Marilyn Monroe, or a list of
all the Republican presidential candidates
of the past twenty years, my mother would
first consult the card index and then
smoothly pull out the appropriate file.
From the stiff paper folders came the smell
of gunpowder and the fizzing sound of
Coca-Cola The Real Thing; Martin Lu-
ther King talked about his dream, Indians
commemorated Wounded Knee in clipped
phrases; you could hear the happy cries of
cheerleaders energetically waving their
bright pompoms, the reverberations of the
shots that killed JFK, the clanking of the
Ferris wheel at Coney Island, and the lonesome teeth-gnashing of prisoners awaiting
execution on death row. When you opened
a folder, rats that had bitten a baby to
death in the Bronx bared their sharp inci-
sors; mobsters flicked their switchblades;
students chanted, *"Hey, hey, LBJ! How
many kids did you kill today?"*; Timothy

Leary was saying that LSD was harmless; corpses with mutilated genitals were being shoved into plastic body bags; blond girls were walking around campus with the cardigans of twin sweater sets slung loosely over their shoulders, piles of books under their arms, telling their boyfriends, teary-eyed, "I'm not ready for it yet, Chad"; and sleazy waitresses slammed umpteen steaks down onto umpteen counters in front of umpteen truck drivers.

In other words, we had everything at our fingertips, right here at home. Without Bureau Van Bemmel, Uncle Sam might as well pack his bags; it was only because my parents snapped the folders shut every evening and wedged them back inside the filing cabinets, like prisoners on death row, that the steaming cauldron that was the U.S. of A. was able to remain intact. A vital element of the sway that we at Van Bemmel held over the United States was the fact that the subject was always plainly identified on the file cover by name and surname, in red ink. "Always label it first," my father used to tell the students. "Only that which is labeled can be retrieved." But I knew there was more to it than that: he was like Adam in the Garden of Eden, who became lord and master of everything by providing every one of God's creatures with the right name. First you saw it; then you named it. Never the other way around. Recognition was key.

Judging from the way my father doted on his files, he would have been happiest, I think, if not a single clipping had ever left the house. He wanted to keep his collection intact. My mother, on the other hand, loved it when the telephone rang and Kes and I had to carry fat packages to the post office after school, assisted by Bas, our receptionist. Bas was a manic-depressive young giant, who would flip from gloom to a wild state of euphoria at the drop of a hat. He stumbled about the house with a heavy gait and called out in his booming voice: "Margje! Margje! Telephone call for Margje!"

My mother's name was Margreet, "Margje" for short, a tender, old-fashioned name, but internationally speaking a disaster. She was sick of always having to spell her name patiently over the phone, and one evening, after we'd been watching *Peyton Place*, when the frozen waterfall came on signifying the show was over, she cried out, "Betty! That's it, kids. From now on I'm Betty Venbemmel."

To make it sound American, she said "Beddy."

Beddy from *Peyton Place* was a wild thing — she lived in a bar. She drank beer straight out of the bottle and hung out with boys, including Norman-babyface, who was a sissy. On that point Billie and I couldn't agree more.

"No-hor-mannnn!"

"Please! I'm going to puke!"

There was nothing different about my mother's behavior in the days following this proclamation, but I didn't trust it for a minute and watched her closely. She was as cheerful as ever. Sometimes you had to ask yourself why she had ever married my father, that silent custodian of his clippings. My father — how shall I put it? — rustled with dry sobriety, whereas she sparkled. People had no trouble adoring her, whether her name was Beddy or not, and I wept into my pillow because she really didn't need to be Beddy at all: not an atom, not a cell, not a filament, not a letter needed improving, in her case. So why did she have to go and tempt fate like that?

My father's name was Frits. He wasn't named after anyone. My grandpa and grandma probably just liked the name.

"Hey, Frits," I once addressed him impudently, lounging against his overflowing desk, "why don't we call it quits?"

He'd slipped his feet off the bottom drawer, which he used as a footrest, sat up straight, and gaped at me shyly.

My father was twenty when he first met my mother. He was studying to become an archivist and was paying his way through college by working in a bicycle repair shop. He'd have liked nothing better than to have been one of the gang, swilling beer and telling dirty jokes along with his fellow students, but every time he tried joining in the laughter, his lips would clench and he'd go stiff with embarrassment. He just didn't have a knack for quick repartee.

He owned one suit and one pair of shoes. He turned his collars himself; he mended his own shoes. In the few photos of him that date from that era, you can tell, from his hungry eyes, how poor he was. Back in those days, he would tell us sheepishly, watching us dunking fistfuls of chips into one of Billie's dips, what he used to dream of was owning a peanut-set — a wooden bowl with six matching little dishes, filled to the rim with fat, crunchy peanuts slick with grease. In his imagination, he would fill his dish from the bowl using a wooden scoop and then toss it down in one gulp.

The phrase "peanut-set" was enough to set us off, Kes and me, rolling on the floor.

Just recently, not long after I moved into our old house, I actually went out and bought myself a secondhand peanut-set, of cloudy gray plastic. I need a preposterous amount of stuff to furnish this house; it's really enormous. They say that your childhood home always seems smaller when you see it again as an adult. But not in my case. Our house seems even larger to me than it did when I was a child, now that there aren't filing cabinets crammed in everywhere.

I saw it in the newspaper. A complete fluke. For sale: No. 11, Lijsterlaan. The letters jumped out at me; the advertisement detached itself from the page and floated up at me, as if it had been meant only for my eyes. It wasn't a matter of choice or of will. The decision had already been made, behind my back, by some higher authority. It was simply one of those coincidences driven by the relentless momentum of fate.

I phoned the real estate agent and, before I knew it, found myself standing beside him on the checked tiles of the entry hall. He was younger than me, naive and

44

wet behind the ears. He went on about the "first-rate location." He clearly hadn't the foggiest notion of what had happened here.

I had prepared myself for a mental show-down. I really didn't know if I was up to it. I set out for the Lijsterlaan convinced that I wouldn't be able to keep my head on straight and that at every step my legs would refuse to comply. I expected the old grief to run me down like a bulldozer. But what actually happened was quite the opposite. I became so incensed at the travesty wrought by the previous owners that I had no time to think about myself. The basement kitchen alone was enough to make your heart bleed. The lovely wooden cabinets had been ripped out, the blue tiles had been painted over, and there were showy built-in appliances everywhere you looked. The whole thing irked me no end. I found myself thinking, What a job it will be to restore everything to its original state — at which point I realized that I had allowed the house to win me over without even the slightest resistance on my part.

On the floors above, too, all traces of us had been thoroughly erased. In the rooms where Esmée and Marie-Louise had once sat hunched over the newspapers, walls

45

had been eliminated left and right. It reeked of the glue, paint, and ink used by the graphic designers whose office had last occupied the space, an unpleasant, impersonal odor. The window in the cubicle adjoining the ground-floor sitting room had been blacked out; this must have been their darkroom. Billie and I used to hang out of that window because from there you had an unimpeded view of Bas's desk.

The real estate agent went over the improvements. The drafty sunroom, where we used to sip our juice after school: torn down. In its place: a soulless construction of aluminum sliding doors. The creaky oak staircase that had been my favorite observation post: replaced by a high-tech spiral contraption of steel. The gas heaters that were so heavenly for toasting your stockinged feet: ripped out. "The central heating is only three years old," commented the agent, glancing at his clipboard.

And at each of his pronouncements I felt a keen little shock of bitter joy, because, in a disconcerting yet irresistible way, the house was reminding me, with each fresh piece of evidence, how happy my childhood here had been, when all was said and done. Strange: nobody has ever suggested

46

the possibility that I might have anything positive to look back on. My past, in other people's eyes, consists only of that one cataclysmic tragedy that took place here. That single day when life blew up in our faces like a time bomb.

The police discovered Carlos and me huddled in the darkest corner of Billie's old cellar, sobbing with fright. Sybille, Kester, and Ida were already dead. They hadn't suffered, apparently. In the forensic lab photos, they looked very peaceful. The same goes for my parents, actually.

While Frits van Bemmel was learning how to make up index cards and dreaming of bottomless peanut-dishes, Margje de Groot was typing out legal briefs in a lawyer's office. She took an apple to work every day for lunch, and a ham or bacon sandwich. These she ate at her desk, which looked out onto a gloomy airshaft. Every Monday morning she purchased six coupons for coffee from the front desk, and six for tea. She never went hungry.

What *her* dreams were remains a mystery, but we do know that she sometimes had the distinct feeling that her life wasn't really her life; it simply could not be, not with that dull little job and those two demanding and tyrannical invalid parents. But she couldn't just leave them to drop dead, either. After work she'd cook some beets or beef stew for those two miserable despots, who could stand neither the sight of each other nor the sight of their daughter, and then go and sit on the little wicker loveseat in her room, trying to stifle the thought that yet another day had been wasted.

Out of pure boredom, she found herself on the verge of getting engaged to a man named Richard who was a fount of botanical knowledge about tulips. They went for a stroll every Sunday. He liked her to wear little white socks.

One Tuesday morning in April, her bicycle had a flat tire on her way to work. She knew of a bicycle repair shop and headed straight for it. This much we know: that she paced impatiently up and down the workshop, which reeked of grease, metal, and rubber. That Frits, every time he looked up from his work, saw her shimmer as a heavenly apparition against the filthy backdrop, in her pastel coat, hands clasped behind her back. She brought the freshness of the early spring

48

morning indoors with her, and it made him think of white sheets, spotlessly laundered, flapping in the wind. She was the kind of girl who inspires that type of imagery: she was as natural and refreshing as a glass of buttermilk. In the summer she would, clearly, have freckles on her arms, and in the winter her cheeks would be ruddy from skating. There was nothing about her to confuse or disconcert him.

Deftly he popped the tire back onto the rim, plopped the bicycle down on the floor, and rode it over to her. "How about going for a ride with me over to Spaarndam on Sunday?" he asked.

She looked up, astonished.

We know that she hesitated.

We know that she was dumbfounded that someone whose name wasn't Richard had noticed her, and that she was subsequently rather disappointed when that person turned out to be our somewhat bedraggled father.

Nonetheless, she said yes. Out of pure contrariness, I should think.

We know that it took Frits Gerardus Theodorus van Bemmel that entire Saturday evening to make his frayed cuffs presentable. We know that he honed his trouser pleats to a razor sharpness over his landlady's steaming kettle. The only thing he couldn't do anything about was the shiny patch on the seat of his pants.

We know that the weather was exquisite the next day: neither a cloud in the sky nor a puff of wind. We know all the facts. We heard them often enough. We can describe precisely, with our eyes closed, how these two people, who were to become our parents, met each other at ten a.m. in the appointed place. At this juncture they are still, no matter how unbelievable it may seem to us in retrospect, two separate individuals with their own separate lives, which means that our unborn infant-souls are still floating free in the cosmos, awaiting our assignment on earth. We ourselves have no contribution whatever to make to the outcome, of course. How can we possibly exert any influence, having neither substance nor heartbeat? Our existence resides only in the fervid hope that somebody down there will welcome us with open arms, that we will be summoned by our true name. Spinning idly through the primal stew of prehuman existence, all we can do is wait and see how, where, and when we will arrive at our final destination. We are pawns in the hands of fate, or, rather, of that which down there is known as love.

Margje's parents were just pouring themselves a cup of coffee that Sunday morning when the doorbell rang. They weren't expecting any visitors. They had made only enough for two cups; they scuttled about the musty kitchen like two old crabs, hands twisted from arthritis, legs hobbled by hardened arteries. Pain and discomfort were their constant companions; they despised their own disabled bodies with a silent, savage hatred. When they looked at each other, they saw themselves and had to look away.

"The bell," she snapped.

He did not reply. He had not yet shaved, a chore he was beginning to dread more and more every day. As she made her way into the hall toward the front door, he observed from the kitchen her ungainly body's waddling gait. She still had curlers in her hair.

"Well, well, Richard!" she exclaimed.

He didn't give a fig for that Richard. He wanted his daughter to marry a lawyer from the firm where she worked.

"Here's Richard," said his wife, stumbling into the kitchen ahead of the guest.

"There isn't any coffee for you," he said nastily. "We weren't expecting you." He

51

nodded at the two cups on the counter.

Richard smiled. He had a symmetrical face and an unusually fine set of teeth. Those teeth were an insult, and the muscles that showed through his shirt didn't help matters either.

"Not to worry. I've only come to fetch Margreet. We made a date for this morning."

"Oh," said Margje's father. He shuffled into the living room and lowered himself laboriously into his corner of the sofa.

Richard immediately took upon himself the role of lackey, carrying in the coffee cups and placing them on the low table. Then he sat down in the chair by the cold gas hearth, folding his hands around his knees. He remarked confidentially, "I don't suppose it would come as a surprise to either of you if I told you I had serious plans regarding your daughter."

She snarled, "I thought Margje said this morning that she was going somewhere with you. To Spaarndam. You and her together."

The father looked up, suddenly interested. It hadn't occurred to him until this moment that his daughter might not be home.

She opened her mouth again: "She left

half an hour ago. To meet you, is what she told me." Her eyes were sparkling with malice.

Bitch, he thought. Bitch. Still, for the first time ever, he felt something close to respect for his daughter. Once Richard had slunk off with his tail between his legs, he thrashed his wife (for never keeping her mouth shut) purely out of habit, for in truth he wasn't really angry at all.

"I thought it was the most decent way," my mother would say in a level voice when she described for us how she had thus managed to dump her beau without an actual confrontation. She looked insufferably coquettish when she said it.

I felt that she made rather too light of it. Had it not been for that fortuitous flat tire on an arbitrary Tuesday morning, Richard might very well have turned out to be none other than my father. In which case half of me would have turned out differently. And how the hell could my parents then have been expected to recognize me as someone named Ellen? My brothers and sisters too would have popped out under different, false names, which would have caused us to flounder hopelessly in the dark trying to figure out each other's true identities. On being introduced, we'd have smiled at each other politely, flashing our perfect teeth.

If you tried really thinking it through, it could drive you nuts. A flat tire, a missed train, a lost handkerchief: it was out of the smallest and most ordinary of circumstances that the entire human race was brought forth! The generations might appear to be joined together in an ostensibly solid chain, but for all we knew, every link in that chain could just as easily have turned out altogether differently. What were we then, we who called ourselves humans? Nothing but a haphazard collection of random genes. God had better help us.

Of course, that was not how our parents saw it when they fell in love. To them it was clear that they had been specially, and with some higher purpose in mind, made for one another: where he was hesitant, she was intrepid; where she would have a fit, he kept his cool. She was spontaneous; he was steady. She could be genuinely offended; he understood the art of compromise. He had ambition; she, compassion. He was a man; she, a woman. A more perfect fit was inconceivable. She had a body. So did he.

By the time they were standing side by side at the altar, there wasn't much point in trying to hide her pregnancy. "Yes I do," they said, and the entire congregation understood what they meant by that. Margje's mother choked on her breath-mint with spite. Next to her sat Richard, who was trying to be a good sport. She heard him exhale with a hiss. It sounded very much like "slut." But perhaps she was mistaken, or perhaps it was only what she herself was thinking. She thought to herself bitterly that she had been right all along, all those times when she'd admonished her arrogant daughter, "Don't think that you are anything special, young lady." Margje wasn't any better or worse than a common streetwalker.

The groom cut a rather listless figure in his rented morning coat. From time to time he shuffled his feet, only to suddenly stand up straight again. Now and then he peeked uncertainly at his wife. He was all too aware that her body betrayed their physical intimacy; the thought made the blood rush to his face. Even though he had never held out much hope for himself in that department, now here it was, conclusive and indisputable: Frits van Bemmel, man of the world.

Behind him he could hear the church-goers coughing and fidgeting. A wave of unrest seemed to be rippling through the church like wildfire, from hard bench to hard bench, as if everyone suddenly saw the same picture in his mind's eye: Margje and Frits, languid and satiated between rumpled sheets. From beneath chaste hats and staid little veils, lewd thoughts suddenly sprang forth; the atmosphere was crackling with it, and many a male hand, as if of its own accord, began to delve deeply into a trouser pocket for a little fumbling down below. The pallid Virgin Mary in the transept hungrily cast her huge eyelids upward; in the stained-glass windows, stiff old saints leaned lasciviously over each other's martyred bodies, and the wooden doves at the foot of the pulpit suddenly began to bill and coo like mad.

Frits blinked and slid the ring onto Margje's finger. It pleased him no end that this didn't do a thing to make her more respectable: the din behind him did not die down for even a second, and there was no need to turn around to know that the two of them, simply by standing there together, had unleashed a veritable orgy. Proudly he placed his hand on her stomach, where Sybille, who had already been waiting a whole six months to be born, began kicking her feet impatiently.

It was Billie who answered my insistent questions and who checked a book out of the library for me. The sight of watery embryos with gigantic heads and defenselessly curled spines gave me a terrible dose of claustrophobia. I deemed it highly unlikely that I myself had ever had to survive that kind of confinement, but it did give me a wicked sense of satisfaction to know that Ida was currently suffocating in there.

After I finished the book, Billie, who was waxing her legs, gave me a further oral briefing on the egg and the sperm. Patiently peeling the last of the sticky wax strips off her shins, she added, business-like, "And you can also prevent it, with a condom."

"Then why don't they?"

"You sound just like Carlos." She held out her hand and I passed her a ball of cotton. Dabbing lotion on her legs, she pronounced, with a dramatic sigh, "The problem is, they can't keep their hands off each other."

"But the question is," said I, all worked up, "whether that's all right with us."

Billie gazed at me with a mixture of irritation and pity. "Get out of here, Ellen; I have to do my armpits."

Billie could be such a prude at times.

I slunk off.

Dog was lying at the foot of the stairs. He stared at me imploringly. Guiltily I went over and sat down next to him. The summer heat hung heavily inside the house. Throughout the office the windows and doors were open wide. "Margje!" Bas roared. "Telephone for Margje, on three."

I heard the tired clumping of my mother's feet. Then her desk chair creaking under her weight. "Beddy Venbemmel speaking," came her voice.

A few moments later she put down the receiver and emerged from her office. She looked pale and worn. "Oh, Ellen," she said with relief, seeing me. "Won't you run over to Marie-Louise's desk to fetch the Orson Welles file for me? I'm just not getting anything done today." She pressed her fists into her back, stretching.

I rose to my feet reluctantly.

Marie-Louise was perched on the corner of her desk, chatting with one of the others. Without interrupting her conversation she looked at me quizzically. "Orson Welles," I said. She took a folder from a stack of files and handed it to me. On my way back, I opened it and looked inside. Thunderstruck, I stopped dead in my tracks. That wide, fleshy face. The dark hair. Those giant drooping jowls. I ran back to my mother's office, slammed the clippings down in front of her, and stormed back out into the hall.

Dog was still sitting slumped exactly as before, at the foot of the stairs, panting heavily. I hauled him into a sitting position, grabbed his right paw and pumped it up and down. Solemnly I said, "Pleased to meet you, Orson." I was so relieved to have discovered his name at last that for the next half-hour I forgot all about Ida, that disaster-in-the-making who was going to be born within a couple of weeks.

# Sybille's first day at the beach, August 1958

I've been camping in the basement ever since I first moved into the Lijsterlaan. There's room enough down here for my bed and for the table at which I do my drafting, drawing my plans meticulously to scale. I'm working my head off. The entire house has been measured and plotted out over the past weeks; every room has been numbered and labeled. I could start calling around for builders' estimates, only I keep coming up with even better ideas. I can't stop scurrying around with my tape measure, my pencils, and my eraser.

There never was much daylight coming through these narrow windows, and there isn't now. When I was a child, being below ground level used to make me feel safe. It was like living inside the belly of a large, friendly animal. That conceit doesn't work for me anymore. The hum of the king-size refrigerator keeps me awake at night, and I can't say that I find the sight of all those stainless steel panels — the oven, the microwave, and the dishwasher — particularly heartwarming.

There is plenty of room here, of course, and it's handy if you're in the mood for a cup of coffee, but what kind of fool sleeps in a kitchen?

Oh, come on, Ellen, enough of that, you knew perfectly well what you were getting yourself into. Make up your mind! Isn't it about time you showed this house who's boss? How about fixing up a proper bedroom for yourself, for a start? In Bas's old office, for instance — why not? It's sunny in there. And it's neutral territory. No need to tackle anything head-on just yet.

All right, all right!

Armed with mops and chammys, I betake myself to what used to be the porter's lodge. The graphic designers left their venetian blinds when they went: couldn't be better. Next I drag my mattress, bedding, and box spring in there. I stack my underwear in neat little piles in the built-in cupboard in the corner. I can't for the life of me remember what Bas used to have squirreled away in there. It is a monumental cupboard. A cupboard befitting Bas's size, Bas with his huge bull's neck and fists as big as coal-scuttles. Bas, the first to arrive every morning and always

61

the last to leave. Bas, the one who had to direct the police to Carlos and me in the cellar. You tend to get so submerged in your own despair that you sometimes forget that the ripples will have touched other people's lives as well.

"Phone call for Margje! Phone call for Margje on three!"

But it's my own telephone that's suddenly ringing, down in the kitchen. Clutching my mop, I listen to it ring, hesitating. Only my doctor knows my new phone number. He insisted on my having a telephone installed. An absolute necessity for when the contractions start, he said. He's an old-fashioned, decent man. The only reading material in his waiting room is an assortment of ancient *Reader's Digest*s. They have this regular feature, "I am Harry's heart," and then, the following month, "I am Harry's adrenal gland," giving you a moving firsthand account of what it's like to be someone's inner organ. Harry doesn't have a uterus, of course, so unfortunately I'll never find out how mine is feeling at this moment, invaded as it is by an exponentially increasing occupying force. But perhaps wombs don't see it that way. Pregnancy is their natural calling, after all.

I throw the mop down in the bucket, run down the kitchen stairs, and grab the receiver: "Hello?"

"Ellen?" says my husband after a few moments' silence.

It has been more than a year since I last spoke to him. How bizarre that I still think of him as "my husband."

"Ellen?" His tone betrays his surprise at finding me at the number he has just dialed.

"Yes."

I hear him breathing. He is mildly asthmatic, nothing to worry about, but enough to provoke constant quarrels about the vacuuming. That everyday, familiar wrangling — You always this, you never that . . . My throat is dry with homesickness. I want to wriggle over to him via the fiber-optic cable and touch that little naked spot under his ear.

"You've received a notice about a Pap smear. The card's been here for weeks. I've been calling all over town, but nobody knew where you were hiding." He articulates every word very carefully, as if he is having a hard time controlling himself. In an even more strained voice he adds, "You can't just go and disappear from the face of the earth like that."

"I haven't. I've been here, home in the Lijsterlaan."

"Home!" It's a shout.

I can picture it: how this morning he suddenly came up with the idea of calling information. His astonishment at the news that a Van Bemmel had indeed recently taken up residence in the Lijsterlaan.

He asks awkwardly, "What on earth are you doing in that big old place?" He really means: What the hell are you up to in that house of ghosts?

I coil the telephone cord around my wrist. Telling him the truth would mean breaking his heart all over again. To meet him halfway I volunteer, almost chattily, "I saw it advertised for sale in the paper. By pure coincidence."

"How much did you pay?" he asks, automatically. He can't help himself. Mention real estate, and you've got Thijs by the short hairs.

Shamelessly, I tell him the price. When I turned twenty-one I came into my share of the estate, consisting of the proceeds of the original sale of the house, wisely invested. Thijs used to say he'd married me for my money. Not that we ever spent a penny of it. Blood money. It remained in the bank, piling up interest. We called it "The

64

Lijsterlaan Fund," an almost mythical nest egg for some unlikely rainy day. Now I've traded it in again for my parental home.

"But your apartment was perfectly nice, wasn't it?" says Thijs, who never set foot there.

"It was too small," I offer feebly.

He is silent. He has never been too good at coming right out with it. Then he says, "I think I'll stop by this evening, to drop off that notice."

Before I have a chance to respond, he's hung up. Agitated, I pull the plug out of the wall. Is it so unreasonable to expect to be left alone at last at the scene of the crime? Who would ever guess that after all these years I would choose to hole up in the lion's den, of all places?

Who else but Thijs, of course, Ellen-authority par excellence, expert interpreter of my motivations, Thijs, who shared my life for thirteen years, blessed with the singular talent of knowing exactly how I wished to be loved. He couldn't have done a better job of it if he'd actually been me. Had he been me, he would also have let me sleep in till noon on boring Sundays, and then woken me with a fresh cup of cappuccino; he'd have supported and assisted me in my work; he'd have put up with my foul moods and never have bought himself an almond cake without spontaneously offering to share it with me.

Poor Thijs, dependable Thijs, repeatedly cuckolded Thijs. Not that the dirty deed ever meant that much to me in itself; it's just that I am addicted to that first, reckless impulse — Hey, you there, your place or mine? — that single, impetuous moment in which you decide to surrender yourself to a total stranger, to someone who might very well be a pervert or a dangerous maniac. That's when you know you're really alive.

I slip on my down jacket and wheel my bicycle out of the shed. It's a bleak, gusty spring day. In the garden daffodils lie broken on the ground, flattened in last night's rain.

It's almost half an hour's ride into town. When I was a child living in the suburbs, it would sometimes annoy me no end to be stuck in the sticks, miles from Haarlem's stores and movie theaters. Those few months I'd attended prep school, all the way downtown in the Prinsenhof, I'd had to cycle my guts out every day just to get there.

As I am chaining up my bike in the

Grote Markt, it starts to rain again, in vicious gusts. Ducking under umbrellas and swaddled in raincoats, people rush past the market stands. I buy fresh tuna, fresh spinach, and some waffle cookies. Feed thy guests; see to it that they want for naught. Only he forgot to mention what time I should expect him this evening. Perhaps some herring, as an appetizer? Or some nuts for my new peanut-set? My mood doesn't improve at the thought. But feed him I shall. I'll make him his favorite mashed potatoes with caraway seeds, and that garlic mayonnaise that's so thick you can stand a spoon up in it. Grimly I buy fresh sage, coriander, and chives, for the salad. Rhubarb, he adores rhubarb. And a bunch of tulips for the table; it's the least I can do.

My shopping bag is bursting at the seams, proof that I bear him no ill-will. Good old Thijs, he wanted me so badly, fourteen years ago. Of the two of us, he is the one who has the right to be angry and disappointed. When I left him, he was literally spent. I had crushed him completely, pulverized him into a pathetic bundle of nerves. He was drinking too much, he gnashed his teeth in his sleep, and during our endless fights he'd acquired this unconscious habit of pulling out his eyelashes one at a time, so that his eyelids were always red and inflamed. Toward the end he often stayed at his office all day and all night.

Thijs is an architect. He has taken on the restoration of historical buildings as his mission in life. Whenever there's an abandoned church or a power plant that's fallen on hard times and is now facing demolition, Thijs is your man. I believe his current project is turning an old water tower at the far end of town into office space for some pension fund. Singlehandedly, he continues to give history a new lease on life; from his drafting table he is able to reverse the laws of cause and effect, giving piles of obsolescent old stone a new *raison d'être* by presenting them with a new function.

I'm sure he'd have preferred to receive any piece of mail in his mailbox other than one reminding him of my reproductive organs. Still, after phoning, he could simply have forwarded it to me, couldn't he, instead of deciding to drop it off in person? Is it that he welcomes the opportunity of telling me face to face that he is completely over me now, that he has met someone else who makes him truly happy? Is he coming to give me absolution, so that we'll be able to think of each other as friends from now on, without cringing?

A lovely thought, although highly unlikely.

Sometimes I have the feeling that Thijs is still out there pelting me with love from our former joint address. Wherever I may roam, I'll always be the north on his compass. I sometimes ask myself what becomes of it, all the love he bombards me with from afar, cubic meter upon cubic meter of dense, solid, reliable love, uselessly glancing off me. And at that point, does all that hopeless, unrequited ardor reveal its true colors — does it turn brittle and fragile? Does it splinter into atoms which then float through the air, invisible to the naked eye, to be inhaled by lovelorn thirteen-year-olds, by homo- and heterosexuals on park benches, at the supermarket, in doorways? *I want you, I want you.* That carnal need, that dire urge to touch the object of one's affection. The overweening greediness and egotism of love — what a deceptive, treacherous thing.

Rainwater drips down inside my collar as I await my turn at the florist's stand. Next to the buckets of cut flowers there are crates stacked with pansies and primroses in riotous colors. There are also peren-

nials: clumps of forget-me-nots, columbine, lavender. There is even a display of
seeds in their shiny packets: nasturtium,
sweet pea, love-in-a-mist.

My sister Sybille used to give me the
creeps by eating nasturtium leaves by the
handful. She'd chew on them blissfully, her
pink cheeks bulging. Billie in a skimpy
summer dress, a little trail of green at the
corner of her mouth. Kester, not wanting
to be upstaged, once bit into a foxglove,
and promptly keeled over, falling flat on
his face in front of us. At first we thought
he was joking; we didn't realize how poi-
sonous it was.

And that's not counting all the trees we
used to tumble out of, the screeching of
brakes as we crossed the road without
bothering to look both ways, the marbles
we stuffed up our noses and the coins we
swallowed, the barbed wire we got tangled
in, the patches of thin ice we skated over,
the bumps and the bruises, the stitches,
the tetanus shots; we survived it all.

"Is that it, for you?" the florist asks,
pointing at the seed-packets I'm clutching.

I shake my head and go to put them
back, but then I change my mind. For it
happens to be the right time of year to do
something about the garden.

Ida was one of those babies who throw up constantly. It began about ten days after she was born: what went in promptly came out again. And it wasn't just a little drool, a discreet belch; that wasn't Ida's way. No: glassy-eyed and waving contorted little fists, she shot out her vomit in one furious jet, as if she was trying to send the stuff into orbit around the earth.

"And what have we got for the pot today then?" cooed Kes, leaning over her. Kes was a real babies' man. He couldn't keep his hands off Carlos either when he was little. Carlos-carlito-carlossus. Idadidda-dya, Idadidda-my-na. His voice squeaky and hoarse. His large boy's hands fondling the little tummy, the wobbly little head carefully supported in the crook of his arm. His zits gleaming with pleasure. Put those two together in a space capsule, and he'd put out enough warmth and she'd generate enough power to light up at least half the Milky Way.

"Just look, Ellen," he said, besottedly, "at those little tiny fingernails."

"How many?" I asked, for his benefit. After all, I was his math coach. *My* report cards always said *Excellent work, Ellen!* and *Well done, Ellen!* I had stolen a large sheet

71

of the card stock my father used for his folders and had propped it at the foot of Kester's bed, with the times tables from one to thirteen written out on it. At some point he'd *have* to learn the difference between zero and a hundred. But Kes had eyes only for Idadidda-dya. He played a tune for her on his musical saw and made a jingly mobile of little ducks to hang over her crib, cut from old cans. His favorite thing was to give her the bottle.

My mother was too tired to feed Ida herself. She hadn't recovered as rapidly from the delivery as she usually did, and I brought her tea and toast in bed, cups of consommé and paper-thin sandwiches. Every morning I'd fling open the curtains in her bedroom and, if that didn't wake her, I'd scuff my feet loudly on the floorboards. Sometimes I brought Orson in with me, because he did what I didn't dare to do: jump right up on her bed, bold as brass. Mama! Beddy Venbemmel! Hey, wake up there!

My father, meanwhile, held the fort at the agency. Watching Billie heat up yet another can of soup for us, he'd say, "We'll just have to improvise for a bit, kids."

Ida, in her cradle, hiccuped, and Kester pounced.

From the moment the vomiting started, she cried all day long. And it wasn't normal crying, it was a howling, an incessant screeching that pierced your eardrums, a hellish bloody murder that never stopped. She bawled from early morning until late at night, and in the wee hours I was afraid her screams would cause the walls to crack, that her ravenous hunger would make the whole house come crashing down.

The doctor advised changing over to a different brand of formula. Ida was a healthy baby; she weighed nearly eight pounds; there was no reason not to take a wait-and-see attitude for another few days. And so our new baby sister kept howling until she was blue in the face, her whole body contorted in fury, arms and legs flailing, her little mouth open wide. Helplessly, we stood on the sidelines, around that gaping hole.

Carlos's bandages had just come off; the little arm poking out of the wide sleeve of his T-shirt was encased in bright red crackled skin. If he caught you looking at it, he quickly hid his arm behind his back. I could tell from his face that Ida's noisy protest scared the living daylights out of him; out of the goodness of my heart I gave him my game of Snap, to cheer him up, but he didn't even thank me. Subdued, he gravely pointed out the clothes he wanted to wear in the morning, the shirt with the flying strawberries and the blue jeans with the worn knees, but you couldn't coax a single *why* out of him anymore.

"*Whehwhehwhehwhenh whehwhehwhehwhenh whehwhehwhehwhehwhehwhenh*," bellowed Idadidda-dya. Her voice had only two tones: rage and despair. Somewhere in the house Esmée and Marie-Louise pointedly slammed their doors shut.

Billie carried her up to Mama. Groggily she took the baby in her arms, her head lolling against the pillows. "Oh but my little bunnikins," she mumbled. In the time that it took Ida to gulp in enough air to fuel her next howling fit, Mama had nodded off again.

Nowhere in the house was safe from her. I sat on the stairs with Orson for hours, unable to move a muscle, held hostage by my confounded sister's piercing wails. At the end of every shriek, the silence would thunder in my ears for a few seconds and the house would seem roomier and lighter. I counted to three, four, five. Then the screeching would resume with a vengeance, as if somebody had given the little key in Ida's back a couple of firm turns.

On the afternoon of the third day, Kester came and sat next to me on the stairs. I didn't even see him; my head felt as if it were filled with Billie's cotton balls; all my brain cells were dried up and corroded. I thought I'd explode if someone didn't put a stop to that caterwauling.

"Nothing wrong with her lungs, anyway," said my brother uncertainly.

I was fiddling with one of the stair-runner's brass rods.

"As soon as she gets tired enough, she'll stop," he said.

"Isn't it time yet for her bottle?"

"Not for another hour."

"Can't you give it to her earlier?"

"No, the doctor said . . ."

"Please, Kes!" Ida's greedy lips tugging at the nipple, milk bubbles popping out of the sides of her mouth. When she was bolting down her bottle she was always convulsed with greed, jerking, slurping, burping, and choking. The wild things in *Where the Wild Things Are* had better table manners than Ida did. She guzzled down her bottle faster than Kester could say peekaboo.

"We've got to wake Mama up. She'll

know what to do about the throwing up."

"Mama has to rest!" said Kester.

"Then Dad'll just have to . . . !" I jumped up. Blindly I ran through the labyrinth that was our house, my heels skidding down the stairs. On the first and second floors all the doors were shut, like faces turned away in rebuke. Behind them people were breathing in and out to the pulsating rhythm of Ida's bawling, but nobody was letting on. Everyone trembled at her ravenous hunger; they were all just as scared as Carlos; they felt there was something unnatural going on. They were probably telling each other, "That child must be possessed!"

"Whoa!" said Bas, as if addressing a horse, when halfway down the stairs I collided with his massive form. He was wearing shorts, with his great hairy legs sticking out underneath. For the first time in days I suddenly realized that the weather was warm; it was summer outside, somewhere. Gruffly, Bas asked me, "Do you secretly pinch your little sister or something, to make her cry like that all the time?"

Alarmed, I looked down. I felt myself blush to the roots of my hair. "Let me through!" I yelled.

I ran to my father's office, my ankles

giving way beneath me, but Dad wasn't at his desk. Esmée said that he was with my mother, to discuss whether Ida shouldn't go to the hospital. "Or she's going to get dehydrated."

At those words, Ida shriveled up in my mind like an Egyptian mummy. She shrank to the size of a pea and then disappeared from sight with an almost imperceptible pop, hurtling back into another dimension, the place she'd come from before she was born. Someday in the future, a flat tire or a missed train might bring two strangers together, and that would give Ida a new, a stronger chance. She would finally be summoned by her true name, and she wouldn't need to be a screeching hole anymore.

Just the thought of it made me sigh with relief. I felt cleansed from head to toe: excused from my role as the evil fairy godmother.

But Ida never did get the chance to escape her unlucky name. That same night, she underwent emergency surgery for what turned out to be a gastrointestinal blockage. They made a new passageway between her gullet and her stomach, and she was going to have to stay in the hospital for seven weeks. The doctors told my father that it had been a close shave. They had never seen an infant with such an iron will: this was a child who was determined to live, whatever it took.

Ida had hardly been gone for more than a few minutes when my mother woke up, just as I was setting her cup of chicken broth down on the night table. Blinking rapidly, she sat up, in a panic. "Ellen! What's going on, for God's sake?"

The question was reasonable enough, but her appearance was another matter: she looked totally discombobulated, her face unnaturally puffy, her hair dull and glued to her skull. She seemed to come around, however, as soon as her gaze fell on the empty cradle at the foot of the bed. "Where's Ida?" she demanded wildly.

"Don't you remember? Dad and Kes have taken her to the hospital. They only just . . ."

Moving sluggishly, my mother clumsily flung back the covers and got out of bed. She was swaying on her feet. Without another word, she began pulling clothes on over her nightgown. A skirt, a blue sweater. Her forehead was beaded with pearls of sweat from the effort.

"Mama," I said in dismay, "shouldn't you take off your nightgown first?"

She pushed me out of her way and marched out of the room, lurching like a robot.

It was six-fifteen and the house was quiet as the morgue. The files were stuffed back into the filing cabinets; the student interns had gone home. It felt as if my mother and I were alone here on earth — an earth that could start spinning and careering out of control at any moment. Suddenly seized by fear, I ran after her. At the stairwell I tried to block her way. "Come on, go back to bed, Mama."

"Out of my way," she said in a throttled voice, flattening me against the wall like a fly. Holding onto the banister with both hands, she started down the stairs on bare feet.

"Where are you going? Mama! Careful! You could fall!" I grabbed hold of her sweater and pulled on it with all my strength. She didn't even seem to notice. With lumbering steps she staggered down the stairs, dragging me along in her wake. My cheek scraped against the rough stucco of the wall, and I let go.

"Billie!" I screamed as loud as I could. "Come quick, Billie!"

My mother was panting; she mumbled something to herself. She had reached the landing and was heading for the next flight.

Where was Billie? Was she lounging in the garden, catching the last rays of sun in her new bikini with the padded cups that cracked us up, Kester and me? The new semester was starting in a few days. It was your last chance if, like Billie, you wanted a chest covered in freckles.

On the first day of school, would my big sister wear the white lipstick that made her look like Jane Fonda? Perhaps it would help me too. I was dreading the prospect of winning over a class full of strangers at my new school. Just to be on the safe side, in case I couldn't come up with anything to say, I had learned by heart every riddle in *Alice in Wonderland. If you divide a loaf by a knife, what do you get? Subtract a bone from a dog: what remains?* Except for the one about the raven and the writing-desk: you'd never catch me trying that one on them. I had asked my father at least a dozen times, "*Why* is a raven like a writing-desk?" But he'd never been able to help me.

"It's a riddle that has no answer," he had tried to explain. "That's the whole joke, don't you get it?"

Well, that wasn't the kind of riddle I was after. *It hangs on the wall and it ticks.* And then you were supposed to say, with a smug grin, *"A dead bird."* If I didn't get what was funny about that myself, how would I ever get them to like me?

"Mama," I yelled downstairs in despair, "why is a raven like a writing-desk?"

My mother stopped halfway down the stairs. She turned around woodenly and gave me a blank stare. Beneath the twisted collar of her sweater I could make out the lace daisy-trim of her nightgown. She gave her head a little shake. The fog was slowly receding from her eyes. "What, Ellen?"

"I don't know why a raven is like a writing-desk!" I began to cry. I ran down to her, two steps at a time.

She caught me in her arms and ran her fingertips over the graze on my cheek. She seemed surprised to find herself standing there with me on the stairs. I was so happy to see her acting normal again that I was sort of half smiling through my tears.

Then she asked, in a perfectly reasonable tone of voice, "Do you know why they've stolen my baby?"

"Ida was taken to the hospital," I sniveled. "Dad came up to tell you so himself! I guess you must have been asleep again!"

She slapped me on the mouth, grabbed me by the collar, and hissed, "Go on, downstairs with you. Go and fetch Sybille. I know she's in on this too. She's already tried to steal your little brother from me."

I hurtled down the stairs, tripping over my own feet.

Billie and Carlos were in the kitchen, playing a game of Snap with my cards. I slammed the door shut, leaning rigidly against it. "Billie!" I managed.

Turning over two cards, she said mournfully, "You win, Carlos."

Squealing with triumph, my little brother deftly pounced on the cards, one on the upper left and one on the lower right, and produced two white rabbits.

Without looking up, Billie said, "Would you mind peeling the potatoes? Dad and Kes should be home any minute." She lit up a Lucky Strike and blew the smoke upward.

I stared at the little raised mole at the corner of her mouth. I knew she'd never believe me if I told her the ugly things my mother had said. Besides, wasn't Mama likely to calm down by herself anyway? She never stayed angry for long. Hesitating, I walked over to the sink and pulled the basket of potatoes out of the cabinet under the sink.

Carlos cried, "Look, Billie, the cradles."

Briskly he flipped the cards over. His left arm was shiny with ointment.

"Lucky for you, pet, isn't it, to have such a dimwit for a sister," sighed Billie.

At that moment the door crashed open and my mother stormed in. "Don't think I don't know what you've been up to, plotting against me behind my back!" she screamed at Billie. She dragged Carlos from his chair, as he squealed frantically, "Mama, Mama!"

I put down the paring knife. The blue tiles over the sink swam before my eyes and the granite counter felt cold as ice under my shaking hands.

"What's the matter?" asked Billie, bewildered. "What's the matter with you, Mama? I didn't even realize you were up."

My mother hoisted Carlos onto her hip and, clutching him tight, shrank backward until she bumped into the stove. Her face was twisted with rage. "Out of my way," she hissed. "I can see through you! You have all . . ."

"What do you mean? Why are you acting like this?"

"You've had me drugged, all this time! So I wouldn't notice my baby was gone! But I'm not crazy, you know!"

Billie slowly got to her feet, her hands

pressing down on the table. She had gone white as a sheet.

"Don't you dare, you," my mother panted, "don't you dare come after my children *one* more time; I won't have it." With a sideways lunge, she snatched the knife from the counter and held it out in front of her.

Carlos twisted his head around anxiously and looked from Billie to me, his eyes open wide. In another moment, he would start screaming.

"Put that knife down," Billie said quietly. "You're scaring Carlos."

My mother's shoulders sagged suddenly; her arm began to shake; she let the knife slip from her fingers, and it clattered onto the tiles. She lowered Carlos carefully to the ground. There he stood, looking up at her sideways, still unsure what was happening. "Oh, Michael, sweetheart," she said hoarsely, "I didn't mean to frighten you."

"His name is Carlos," I whispered under my breath.

My mother wiped her eyes.

Billie walked silently over to the sink, moistened a dish towel, and handed it to her. Mama pressed the towel to her forehead. She sat down at the table. The red patches in her neck gradually began to fade.

As if by some prearranged signal, Billie and I both turned toward the sink and began cleaning the beans and the lettuce. I gazed down at the little blond hairs on Billie's bare forearms. My own were still standing on end. Shaking, I held the colander with the lettuce under the tap. The citizens of Attica used to spice their food with marjoram and cumin; wine was cheaper than oil; there is no evidence that the Greeks, even in the northern regions, knew about fermented beer; the Spartans' daily diet consisted of nothing but a bowl of black soup.

Behind me, Carlos was saying, "Look, Mama, I've got so much more pairs than Billie."

"Clever boy," my mother answered in an unsteady voice. I heard her getting up. A moment later I felt a timid hand on my shoulder. "What big girls I have," she said. I turned around. She looked exhausted and ashamed. She gave me a clumsy kiss and then turned to Billie. "Sybille, I hope you will —"

We heard the front door open and close. Kester and my father walked in, and all at once the kitchen was filled with their noisy relief. That Ida was quite the little trooper; everybody at the hospital had said so. "We can all be proud of her," said my father, putting his arm around Mama's waist and pulling her close. He rattled on without pausing for commas for at least five minutes, about the diagnosis, the surgery, and the recovery — which was expected to be brief. It was the longest single sentence he had ever uttered in his life.

My mother listened with a frown of concentration. "So then it wasn't because I didn't nurse her myself? I was so tired. I could only —"

"My darling, it's a congenital defect. You don't need to feel guilty about any of it. But wouldn't you like me to fetch you your robe? What kind of a getup is this you've got on?"

"We can visit her every day," said Kes. He inspected the contents of one of the pans hungrily. "We're not having soup again, are we?"

My mother squared her shoulders. "From now on, I'm going to take charge around here again. All that snoozing in broad daylight, that's fine for foreigners, or for pets." She shot Billie and me an urgent look of apology. "I just don't know what came over me. But it's all over and done with, agreed? Now please clear away those Snap cards, then we can sit down and eat."

That night in bed I tried to record in my journal what had happened, but written down in black and white, my mother's outburst seemed even more implausible. It just wasn't like her, to lose it like that. She'd just been in an angry mood, and because of my frayed nerves the last few days, I had blown it out of all proportion. I tore the whole page out of my diary, turned to a clean one, and, for my list of possible topics of conversation, wrote down everything I knew about the life cycle of the whale, and the care and feeding of large black dogs.

When Thijs and I were still married, he was always the one to mow the lawn. Sometimes he would come down with a case of green-thumb fever, and then he'd spend the entire weekend digging the dandelions out of the grass as if possessed. I myself was more the type to sit back and serenely contemplate the honeysuckle, a glass of white wine within reach. But now, if I want to see something done about the sadly derelict yard of the Lijsterlaan, I'll just have to roll up my sleeves. Weeds are poking up between the flagstones of the terrace, the ivy has put out creepers a mile long, in the back the weeds and nettles are knee-high, and the pond is choking with green scum. Look a little more closely, and the picture is even more devastating. Bindweed is rampant in the flower borders; crabgrass has invaded at least fifty percent of the lawn. It's a jungle of menacing green out there, far more vigorous than the poor seeds I just bought in the market.

This is not just some little job; this is a project. But if there's one thing I have plenty of these days, it's time. All I need is some gardening tools.

I put the tuna and rhubarb I bought for Thijs in the refrigerator and head for the garden center that has sprung up in the neighborhood. A spade, a rake, some hedge shears, a weedkiller for the grass, bags of compost, gloves, a hoe, pruner, wheelbarrow. You can think small, a few packets of seeds, or you can go for something a little more extravagant.

I navigate my brimming shopping cart along the narrow aisles with some difficulty. It's hot in my tight jeans. It won't be long before I'll have to wear something a little roomier. Pregnancy is a funny thing. You're just like an apple or a pear: you've got no choice; you're forced to ripen. The decision isn't yours, no matter which way you look at it. I wonder how my mother took it. I've been thinking about her a lot lately. About the way she must have felt while expecting us. We know she was equally overjoyed with all five of us. My father no less. One of their joint rituals was to paste family photographs into albums, and they did this religiously every New Year's Day, beaming with pride, laughing and arguing about the exact date and what caption to write underneath.

My mother would wear her hair pinned up in an untidy knot; my father would play with the little tendrils escaping at her neck.

When they'd finally finished and we were permitted to inspect the album, sipping a cup of hot aniseed-flavored milk, Mama would say dreamily, "What a good-looking bunch of kids you are. Look at this one of you, Billie, and you, Kester . . ."

"That's because you all look like your mother," remarked my father.

"Not me," I said anxiously. "I look like you, Daddy."

"That's because you're the third child, sweetheart, just like me," he said and he gazed at me so gravely over the top of his glasses that my heart swelled with pride.

At the information booth by the exit, I ring the bell. What a smoothly run operation this garden center is. Do you have any questions before you leave the premises? We shall be glad to answer them for you.

Immediately a bear of a man in a red jacket pops up behind the counter, his hair pulled back in a ponytail.

"I'd like to have this delivered to my house," I tell him.

Without looking at me he gets out a form and a pen. "Certainly, madam. We can even get it there today if you like, but it will have to be after four."

"That's fine. Van Bemmel, 11 Lijsterlaan."

His pen slips, scoots across the page. He looks up. And that is when I recognize him, across the chasm of time. I almost give in to the impulse to run, but he has grabbed my arm across the counter; his giant hand has me pinned. *"Ellen?"*

The wrinkle on the bridge of his nose has turned into a groove. He was twenty-four when I was twelve: he must be in his late forties now. Quickly I say, in the neutral voice of someone who has a very busy life, "I can't believe it — Bas! How *are* you?"

"Fine." His face breaks into a smile.

"What a surprise. I didn't know you had moved back —"

Quickly I try to distract him. "You're looking well, I must say."

"Yes indeed, in me you see the living proof of the miracle of Prozac."

"Have you been working here long? Quite a change from . . ." Immediately I wish I hadn't said that.

"I've thought about you often, Ellen. About all of you."

I begin to sweat. He is well aware that, twenty-five years ago, it had been intended that I would kick the bucket too. Like my brothers and sisters, I wasn't ever supposed to grow up. "Look, I've got to run," I say abruptly.

"Just a minute, your receipt." He scribbles my name and address on the ticket. "I just wanted to say . . ."

"Perfect." I'm practically gasping for breath.

"And that's why I sent you that postcard, that time. Do you remember?"

A postcard plops out of a secret drawer in my mind, a postcard with a picture of the Keukenhof flower gardens, and, scribbled on the back: *Wrm grtngs and all the best, Bas.* I can even picture the thumbtack that fastened it to the wall over my bed in the Unicorn; the white plastic head had come off, and a rusty smear had eventually oozed over the tulip fields, a thin circle of reddish-brown that looked like dried blood.

To my horror I feel the tears coming on. I turn and run, blindly crashing into people and shopping carts until I've left the store far behind me.

At first I thought of it as a kind of summer camp. There were children of all ages, and bearded group leaders who wore bandannas around their heads, read *The Lord of the Rings*, and rolled their own cigarettes.

Carlos and I were housed in the Unicorn. There were five other identical buildings that looked like bungalows. They all had flat roofs and French doors. They were called "pavilions," a word I'd come across before only in *A Thousand and One Nights*.

For the first time in my life I had my own room, with yellow curtains and a checked bedspread, and on our arrival I gushed to Carlos, "It's really posh here!" We would drift around the extensive grounds all day, wandering under the old linden trees, or we'd play croquet with

Sjaak, our group leader, who brandished his mallet as if he were about to fell an ox. Marlies and Gerda, two big girls with common accents and yellow hair who both wanted to become models, taught me to play poker, and when the weather was hot we'd run screaming through the sprinklers in our bathing suits. I was quite a hit with my tales of the lovely Helen and the Trojan horse, and I was a paragon of industry when it came to doing the dishes. If nobody else could think of something fun to do, I'd do my impression of squeaking rats biting a baby to death or I'd tell them stories about mobsters throwing each other into the sea with blocks of cement on their feet. I had no idea myself where those stories came from; my head was simply a bottomless storage jar. Sjaak would sometimes pinch me by the scruff of the neck and tell me I really didn't need to try so hard. And that it really hadn't been necessary to give Carlos half of my earthworm.

Several times a week my little brother and I had to go see a woman called Marti in her office and produce drawings for her. Carlos, who was still only at the coloring stage, didn't sweat it, but I'd draw a perfect Orson for her every other day, black and hulking and huge. Sometimes I'd spend as much as half an hour on the shape of his ears or the precise curl of his tail. If a portrait turned out particularly well, I would ask Marti to send it to the kennel, so they could hang it above his cage. That way everyone could tell that he had an owner, and nobody else would take him home by mistake before the end of the summer.

"Do you miss Orson so much, too?" Marti asked my brother.

Lips sealed, he just went on with his coloring. I would sometimes shake him mercilessly when nobody was looking, hoping to activate his voice box. All the *whys* had died on his lips.

Marti, with her sweet angular face, said it was just a matter of time. Carlos would start talking again when it suited him, and if I had any questions or anything I wanted to get off my chest I could always come to her. She wasn't all that good at drawing, but she did sketch me an airplane once. It had a long wavy pennant floating after it that read: "ELLEN VAN BEMMEL FOR PRESIDENT." She asked me if it reminded me of anything, looking at me expectantly. I told her that if a plane like that ever flew very low over the Netherlands, everyone would know my name, as if I were Mick Jagger.

She put the drawing away with a disappointed look on her face. I felt so bad about giving the wrong answer that I got a stomachache. I had cramps that whole day. I was really feeling too ill for the treasure hunt Sjaak had organized for us that evening to celebrate his birthday, but I was afraid of letting him down as well.

We had been out in the dark woods for only fifteen minutes, training our flashlights on the bits of metallic ribbon Sjaak had hung from the tree branches, when I suddenly felt a terrible need to pee. Squatting behind a bush, I happened to look down at the crotch of my panties. It scared the living daylights out of me at first, but then a little lightbulb went on in my head. I stuffed one of my socks awkwardly into my soiled undies and ran to catch up with the others. By this time my stomach really hurt, and after only half an hour of walking I had a huge blister on my heel. We caught a glimpse of a deer strutting in a clearing, innocently showing off its beauty, but I'd much rather have been in bed.

Back at the Unicorn, I buried my soiled panties at the very bottom of the laundry basket. There were sanitary napkins in the linen closet in the hall. I had once seen Marlies grab one from there. I pulled on a clean pair of underpants over the pad and went to bed miserable. I suddenly missed Orson so much that as far as I was concerned they could have taken the rest of my vacation and shoved it.

Early the next morning I asked Sjaak if I could have some condoms. He said, No way, have you lost your marbles, Ellen, and can't you stop begging for attention all the time?

Thoroughly confused, I slunk away. When you got your period, that's when you started having babies, and if you didn't want any, you had to use a condom. Billie had said so herself.

I felt as if I'd been punched in the solar plexus with a croquet mallet; I found myself gasping for air. But then the shutter that had opened just a crack to reveal a glimpse of that ghostly apparition slammed shut again. I didn't even know any Billie.

Knees trembling, I went to find Marti and told her that in ancient Rome the girls were always given a condom when they first started having their periods, and wasn't that a sensible custom. Marti thought it over. Then she nodded, to my great relief.

She pulled out her bottom desk drawer, took out a little blue packet and held it up.

"See? They're here for you whenever you need one. Once you have a boyfriend, you can come and get one any time you like. But Ellen, there's plenty of time for that yet, you know. How old are you now . . . twelve? Nearly thirteen?"

I nodded.

"Well, know what I'll do? I'll keep them here for you. Isn't that a good solution?"

"As long as I don't have to have any children," I told her severely.

"Why not?" she asked with great interest, picking up her pen.

Suddenly I was conscious again of that shutter at the back of my head. It was as if something were knocking on it urgently. Confused, I looked down at the tips of my shoes. Then I had it. "Orson doesn't like babies," I said.

Marti put her pen down. "Then let's go and visit Orson, shall we?"

We took the bus. It was a lovely clear day, but you could smell that summer was already past its prime. Pretty soon, you'd be able to see the early-morning spiderwebs outlined with dew, ripe for scooping up from the bushes with twigs bent into loops.

I had brought a bone for him as big as

my arm. Around my wrist was the charm bracelet Marti had given me. I loved it so much that I had to force myself not to wave my hand around constantly to see it sparkle.

The kennel was tucked away on the outskirts of the city, down a muddy lane. The smell of piss and dog food hit you in the face as you entered. At the end of the corridor was a screen door through which I could make out a room full of cages. A great tumult went up. "Orson!" I bellowed over the barking.

"Take it easy now," said Marti.

A young girl in a rubber apron was sweeping the floor. She said sourly, "Orson is in the outdoor run."

The ground was so muddy I nearly slipped. Out in a paddock I saw a swaybacked pony. Then I caught sight of my dog. He had the entire run to himself, but he was just lying there sadly, stretched out in the dirt. There were a couple of dented feed bowls in the corner.

I didn't even have to call him. His ears pricked up as soon as he heard my footsteps; he sprang to his feet, all four paws leaving the ground at once, worked himself into a gallop, and threw himself against the fence with a dull thud, wagging his tail and yelping with joy. He tried to lick my face right through the chain links.

"Hey! Watch out there! That dog is dangerous!" A man in big rubber boots came rushing over.

"But I know him," I said. "He's mine."

The man paused. Then he asked curiously, "Oh, so you must be one of the —"

Marti cut him short. "Can't we let him out for a bit?"

"No, but she can go in, if she dares. By the way, it looks as if we're never going to find a taker for this dog; he's been here far longer than thirty days already, so will you . . ."

Inside the dog run I threw my arms around Orson's neck. I pressed my nose into his dense fur and inhaled his comforting old-raincoat smell. It really was him. And then I realized that I'd been half afraid, all this time, that I had just made him up; that he might not really exist. How could I ever have thought that! Together we rolled around on the ground, yelping with delight. I pulled his ears back so that he looked like an overgrown hamster and scratched him between his faithful eyes. His coat was all matted, or perhaps it was ticks, and on his back there was an ugly bald spot. It would take quite a bit of work to make him presentable again.

Marti looked on, her fingers hooked through the wire links of the fence. After a while she asked, "Ellen, do you remember when you first got Orson?"

"On my twelfth birthday," I said without thinking.

"And who gave him to you? Do you remember?"

"He came from the pound."

"But who picked him out for you?"

I pushed Orson away. Suddenly I didn't feel like playing with him anymore. But he wouldn't stop yelping and squealing and butting me with his head. I took the bone from the greasy bag and tossed it halfheartedly across the dog run. Silly waste of time. Crazed with excitement, the dog just kept coming at me, the bone clenched between his teeth, his eyes beseeching, Come on, throw it again, Ellen, throw it. The stupid creature just didn't know when to stop. "All right now, enough, down!" I snapped. Meekly he sank to the ground, his tail drumming on the earth. I quickly slipped out of the run and pulled the gate shut behind me.

Marti placed a hand on my shoulder and asked softly, "Do you remember it now, Ellen? Who it was who picked Orson out for you?"

I had wanted a cute little puppy, not a big fat unruly brute that knocked you off your feet all day and never knew when to stop. A hand-me-down to boot. "Let's just go," I said.

Actually, we did have another dog before Orson: Billie had a poodle when she was little. I don't know what happened to it; I don't even remember its name. It was probably before my time — I suppose I got to know it only from the photos in the family album with the tissue paper between the brown pages.

You can see the dog in the snapshot of Billie's first day at the beach. My sister looks to be about a year old in that picture. The dog is sitting beside her in the sand, an absurdly adorable thing. Scheveningen Pier hazy in the distance. The wicker beach chairs. The sea torpid on the horizon.

My sister is clutching her little dog by the curly scruff of its neck. The dog, for its part, is looking expectantly at my mother, who is holding a picnic basket on her lap and is smiling somewhat vaguely at the beach photographer's camera, as if her thoughts are on the thermos of oxtail soup she packed this morning.

It's a blustery day, there's a stiff breeze blowing, and the sky is gray. Still, my father, with the obstinate intrepidness of the Dutchman on his day off, is wearing shorts, the wide cuffs flapping against his thighs. The wind has blown the hair into his eyes. His calves are smarting from the sand. He is leaning forward and saying, "Shall I take Sybille in for a little wade, or did you want to eat first?"

She brushes the back of his knee with the inside of her wrist. "No, go ahead." She flashes him a languid, tender smile. Last night before going to bed she watched him hover over his daughter's crib with a rapt expression on his face, and she could tell that in his thoughts he was filling Sybille in about the sea, the impudent seagulls, the beach that faced England across the waters. She had been moved, and also just a tad amused: he may be the silent type, but she reads him as easily as a knitting pattern. A man who can't wait to show his daughter the sea.

He picks Sybille up from the sand. The poodle jumps up, barks, then lies down again.

Frits feels his daughter's sandy legs clenched around his waist and he presses her cheek into his neck, pulling her ruffled sunbonnet straight. She gurgles something and bangs both hands on his shoulder.

"Yes-yes," he says affectionately. He carries her toward the shoreline, saying Yes-yes every now and then, Yeah, little girl, All right, yes. How easy, how straightforward the interaction with a very young child! Here's your daddy, little girl. Contented little creature with your clear gaze and your cooing sounds. It would never occur to you to call me names like stuffed shirt, nincompoop, stick-in-the-mud. To you I am the biggest and mightiest thing in the universe; you have made a hero of me, a knight in shining armor. Love me forever and ever.

He trudges slowly, unhurriedly through the wet sand. Only where the water starts lapping at his ankles does he turn around and wave at Margje.

"Hee!" shouts his daughter, thrashing in his arms.

He wades out farther. They both scream in unison as a wave splashes up to his chest. Their cheeks are splattered with salty water. "Steady now. Daddy's holding you tight." He folds his big hand around an icy little foot. They are standing together in the gray, never-ending sea. Very gently, it starts to rain.

There's no way he'll ever be able to love a second child as much as he loves Sybille. But Margje wants to have six. She has happy visions of a house filled with laughter and noise. A round table, surrounded by eight chairs. Bulging cheeks blowing out birthday candles. Oh, come on, Frits, you know how awful it was for me, growing up as an only child.

He thinks of her breasts, already swollen again, and tells himself: That's the first sign, and is overcome with unexpected delight at this secret knowledge, the delicious intimacy it implies. Three girls and three boys, every one as dark-haired and fair-skinned as his wife, squabbling, shrieking with laughter. Chocolate milk, splinters in stubby little fingers, sleepy heads nodding on his shoulder.

Margje's dreams will definitely come true, because so far they always have. To be married to someone so indomitably driven by inner conviction can be quite a challenge. What you're dealing with is something bigger and mightier than yourself: you simply have to accept her confidence and her faith in you, her unshakable belief that you have something special to offer, that you will be able to give your kids a blessedly happy and carefree childhood.

★ ★ ★

The bell rings just as I'm halfway through my second eye. My mascara smudges. It's too early: could it be Thijs?

It's Bas.

The red blazer has been traded in for a blue windbreaker.

Caught off guard, I stare at him.

"I just came by to say that I didn't mean to upset you this morning," he blurts out. He rubs his thumb against the side of his nose, a gesture I suddenly remember from my childhood.

"That's all right. Don't worry. You needn't —"

"No, really, I mean it. I'm sorry."

I shift my weight from one leg to the other. The situation is so awkward.

"Well, that's it, really. I'll see you at the Garden Center one of these days perhaps." He extends his large hand. "Bye, Ellen."

"Bye."

He turns and walks down the garden path. His ponytail is bunched inside his collar. At the gate, he leans over his bicycle to unlock it, then he tucks the bottoms of his pants carefully into his socks. I had no idea people still did that. On an impulse I run after him and pull at his sleeve just as he's getting on his bike. "Thank you for having my things delivered."

"Oh, no big deal." The familiar way he shrugs his mountainous shoulders. Kester and I used to imitate him behind his back, muttering under our breath, *"No big deal. No big deal."*

There's no one else left who knew me as a child. Nobody else who remembers my first bicycle, my drawings that were displayed in the stairwell, my red sandals with the buckles. Nobody else who witnessed my mother drawing me onto her lap to push my hairclips neatly back into my hair while talking to a client on the phone. No one who saw my father laughing at my joke about Sam and Moos meeting in the main street. He'd laughed so hard that his glasses fogged up. He had lifted me up on top of his desk piled high with files and said, "Tell it again, Ellen."

Bas is my only witness.

It is at this moment that Thijs suddenly appears around the corner. He must have left his car at the riding stable and come on foot the rest of the way. He strides up to us briskly. He is wearing a snappy checked jacket I've never seen before and toting his old briefcase. Also a bunch of roses.

Instinctively I pat my hair. Be still, fluttering heart. It's only our ex.

"Oh," says Thijs, looking from Bas to me, "I think I've come at a bad time."

"Not at all," says Bas. "I was just going."

"Thijs Kamerling," I introduce them. "Bas Veerman."

"Hi," Bas smiles. "And good-bye." He gives a wave and leaps on his bike, surprisingly nimble for such a heavy man.

Thijs and I just stand there for a few moments on the front steps. Then I say, "Ellen van Bemmel, how d'you do?"

"Well, well, stranger!" He is equally jovial. But he looks better than he has looked in years. The lines of pain and bewilderment have faded from around his mouth. His eyelashes have grown back. He looks himself again, the self he was before he fell into my clutches.

From an oak branch right above our heads, a spring-crazed chickadee sets up an earsplitting chirping. Thijs looks up. I notice that he has just shaved, and I wish I could trace the smooth throat under his collar with my fingers, undo the topmost button of his shirt and loosen his tie a little, just for the thrill of that casual touch, the intimate touch that is the everyday prerogative of the loved one. The loved one I have chosen no longer to be.

Thijs tears his eyes away from the tree

and fixes his gaze on me. We are the same height, he and I. I've never been able to imagine what it would be like to be married to someone taller or shorter than myself. "You've gained a little weight," he says. "Suits you." The roses he is hugging to his chest wink at me. At least two dozen, I estimate, at a glance. He has always been generous, a quality I hold dear; he considers his fellow man worth his time, his attention, and his cash.

"Shall we go in?" I suggest.

"Oh, no," he says to my dismay, "no, I don't want to put you to any trouble — I happened to have some business in this neighborhood tonight anyway, so . . ." He brings up his knee, balances his briefcase on it, the calfskin briefcase that I bought him several years ago in a fit of contrition and remorse, and takes out a postcard. "Here's that notice."

"Don't you want a drink or something?" The words pop out automatically.

"No, really, thanks." He pins the roses under his arm so they won't fall as he clicks his case shut. He avoids my eyes.

"Don't tell me you don't have the guts to step inside this house."

He stands up straight. "Ellen," he says, somewhat wearily, "I spend my entire day working inside buildings haunted by all *sorts* of ancient tragedies."

To stop him from leaving, I ask, "How's your work going? I was reading something about that water tower . . ."

"Fine. And yours?"

"Me? Oh, I'm on unpaid leave for a while. A sabbatical of sorts. I just needed a rest."

He gives a quick glance up at the house. All the windows are covered, thanks to the graphic designers' venetian blinds.

I point up at the dormer window. "That's where I used to sleep."

He ignores the bait. "You mean the lab let you go off just like that?"

The world I've left behind like a thief in the night is so unreal to me now that the word "lab" means nothing to me at first. Then, suddenly, the smell of formaldehyde comes back to me; I remember what unyielding dead flesh feels like beneath the scalpel. Most people consider it a rather macabre line of work, but I've always liked it. It's methodical, tidy, circumscribed. "Sure," I say. "Willem had no problem with it." Immediately I wish I could bite off my tongue. Thijs does not have fond memories of Willem.

"Well," he says, "you've got everything

worked out just splendidly, I see." He fumbles with the roses and his briefcase, planning his escape.

"Thijs?" I say it without a clue what to say next.

He brings up a hand and starts plucking at his eyelid. "I'll give you a ring some time."

"I'd like that."

"OK, then, see you."

"Sure," I say, defeated. "Bye."

Without looking around, he walks back in the direction of the riding stable. Which leads me to the conclusion that the roses must indeed have been meant for me, for wouldn't he have left them in the car otherwise?

In the hallway mirror I stare at myself despondently. What did I do wrong? Oh, shit, that smear of mascara under my eye makes me look wanton, disheveled, as if I've just come from a roll in the hay. With Bas. That's Ellen for you, Thijs must have thought, she hasn't changed one bit.

For one feverish moment I consider phoning him as soon as he gets home. But what's the point? In a few weeks I won't be able to show myself to him anymore anyway. And besides, I don't need his love: I have nothing, absolutely nothing, to give him in return. Billie was right when she said, "That boy isn't your type, Ellen." He has always expected far too much of me. And if you have any expectations, you shouldn't come knocking at *our* door. We are allergic to expectations, Kester, Sybille, and I.

# Ida's christening,
## 4 September 1972

I'm lying on my back with my legs in the stirrups gazing up at the crumbly ceiling tiles of Dr. Bramaan's examination room. It's such a seedy practice. In the waiting room the chrome on the furniture is speckled with age and the fake leather seats are crazed with fine hairline cracks. It's always crowded with stocky Turkish or Moroccan women, often accompanied by some eight- or ten-year-old acting as their interpreter. There are Dutch women too, to be sure, with bruised faces or perhaps other less visible injuries.

Bramaan, not a man to stand on ceremony, calls us in by our first names. Lucia! Fatima! Ellen!

I've seen Lucia here twice already, Fatima too. They always look pale and worn-out. As I read about Harry's spleen or pancreas, I am aware of their openly hostile eyes taking in my leather jacket, my smart new designer handbag, my cool suede shoes. I am an outsider, an interloper in Dr. Bramaan's office: someone who could easily afford a fancier doctor.

Lying on the examination table I feel him probing. Bramaan surfaces from between my knees, his wide, bald head red with exertion. "All done," he says in his clipped country accent. He switches off the lamp that, wobbling at the end of a rather rickety arm, had been lighting up my crotch.

I sit up.

"Everything looks fine." He throws his gloves into the sink; in the narrow confines of the examination room, I bump against his hip as I pull on my panties.

In his office he sits down, sighing heavily, at an oak desk emblazoned with water rings. "Anything else?"

"No," I say. "I hardly notice I'm pregnant."

"Well, it is a natural condition, after all," he says. He scribbles something on my chart. "Would you like a sonogram?"

"What for?"

"That way you'll have an early snapshot."

I have to laugh.

"What about a midwife?"

"No, I'd rather stay with you." I can just picture how he'll manage my delivery: silently, painlessly, both of us drenched in sweat and deeply moved, and no complications.

He nods. "If you start to retain water, you should switch to a salt-free diet right away. But you're a doctor yourself; you know what to watch for. All right then, see you in four weeks."

"Bye, doctor." I like him. He looks like the sort who would help himself to a good deep inhalation of ether at the end of the day and enjoy it with a clear conscience.

Outside it is sunny and warm. Children dart around me, playing hopscotch on the steps. It's Friday afternoon, and there's a festive holiday feeling in the air. It's a fine day for an outdoor café.

I stroll over to the Grote Markt. The square is a sea of chairs and tables littered with bottles and glasses. I stake out a strategic spot, put on my sunglasses, and undo the top button of my blouse. At the table next to mine a man is deeply immersed in his book. I cross my legs and dangle my shoe from my big toe, tilting my face up to the sun.

I'm thinking of the sullen faces of Lucia and Fatima and trying to imagine what their lives are like, when I hear a voice asking me if the chair next to mine is free. Without opening my eyes I nod. The voice orders a Campari and soda. "And perhaps the lady would like one too?" A confident voice.

"Thank you," I say.

While we are waiting for our drinks, I am offered a cigarette. I inhale deeply, with just a twinge of guilt toward my womb.

He starts off with a comment about the lovely weather. I remark that it's a good thing for the art of conversation that there's always weather of some sort to talk about. I push my sunglasses up into my hair. He tells me about his sailboat. There's always either a boat or a Harley, or else they're into extreme sports. And these days, you often have to listen to a lot of high-tech gibber-jabber as well.

"By the way," he interrupts himself when we're onto our second drink, "the name's Johan."

I glance at him. I never pay too much attention to the face.

"Sybille," I say.

"Do you have any plans for tonight, Sybille?"

I raise my arms over my head and stretch. He smiles, his teeth digging into his lower lip. "How about a ride to the beach?"

I suppose that means we'll first have to

eat fish in Zandvoort, watch the sunset, and God knows what other little rituals. I sit up and, to hurry things along a little, lightly touch his chest. A bodybuilder, this Johan. When one of these lands on your gurney, it's quite a job. You have to dig uncommonly deep with your scalpel to get to the heart. Willem, my boss at the forensic lab, likes to say that because we spend so much time with the dead, our vital urges are stronger than those of other people. Eros and Thanatos.

I don't really buy his theory. Still, any excuse will do. "Well, let's go then, shall we?" I say.

※　※　※　※　※　※

Since according to Billie I could be starting to sprout breasts at any moment, I examined my chest thoroughly on waking up every morning. My disappointment was always tempered with relief: I knew Kes wouldn't be seen dead with me at the swimming pool if I had to start wearing the same kind of swimsuit as my sister. He would leave me to my own devices in the great green-tiled pool where those gangling bullies dunked you the moment the lifeguard was looking the other way.

It certainly was a big load off my chest when the end of September came around and the swimming pool closed before I was ready for padded cups. Time for Carlos and me to get our blowpipes out and fire berries and rose hips through open windows, or to cobble together wobbly little men out of horse chestnuts and matchsticks, with an acorn-cap skewered onto their knobbly heads by way of a hat. Acorns were superabundant that year, and my mother paid us five cents for every jelly jar filled, so they wouldn't sprout and take root on the lawn.

I went on a fall field trip to the moors with my new class and sprained my ankle because as we were getting off the bus someone shoved me from behind and I fell off the bottom step. The biology teacher with the bushy mustache insisted that my classmates take turns carrying me two by two over the bumpy terrain on their interlaced hands. But as soon as he sank to his knees before an awesome specimen of fly agaric, they started hissing "crybaby" and "sissy" in my ear. I was saved by a trick Kester once taught me: you tickled the roof of your mouth with your tongue. That was the way the American Indians stifled the tears or sneezes that might give them away.

Nobody at this prep school even knew who Chief Seattle was, or that John Wayne's real name was Marion Michael "Duke" Morrison. They were a hard-boiled bunch of grinds; all they were interested in was *amo, amas, amat* and prancing around in their navy school pullovers, with the motto *"SOL IVSTITIAE ILLVSTRA NOS,"* which you were supposed to wear in this geeky way, with the sleeves draped over your shoulders and knotted in the front.

Just as I was starting to get the hang of the ablative case, Ida came home from the hospital, weighing twelve pounds.

Esmée had bought her a felt elephant that had little bells dangling from its ears, and Marie-Louise had picked some asters for her from the planter on her balcony. Welcome home, Ida. None of us had thought of getting her a present ourselves, as if we'd already forgotten her.

"No, Ellen, you're wrong," said my father. "It was just that we didn't dare hold out so much hope." I suddenly noticed that his hair was gray at the temples.

The day after Ida's homecoming, my mother called me up to her room very early in the morning. She was hovering over the cradle at the foot of the bed in her robe. Dad was still asleep. "Look, Ellen, look at the shape of her head, does it seem right to you?" she whispered.

We considered Ida's well-fed little head on the white pillow. She was fast asleep; her eyes were squeezed shut.

My mother said, "No, see, I mean, shouldn't it look more like this?" Placing her open palms against Ida's cheeks, she squeezed gently. The baby lips bulged out in an exaggerated pout.

"I don't know, Mama. She's just a little fatter."

Our discussion made my father sit up in the big bed. He peered around myopically. He gave off a sour smell, a smell of stale breath and unconsummated dreams. I was suddenly overcome with shyness. "What's the matter, Ellen?" he asked helplessly, fumbling for his spectacles.

"Nothing. I'm going down to set the table for breakfast, all right?"

Downstairs I swiftly doled out plates and bowls.

Billie came shuffling in. Grumpily she demanded, "What's a parallelepiped?"

"A prism of some kind."

"Oh. I thought it was something to do with parallelograms."

"That as well. Wait, I'll draw it for you."

"What's the point of that?" she said indignantly. "I mean, I don't have to *under-stand* it, do I? All I need from you is the answer."

"Ellen," complained Carlos, coming down barefoot and in his pajamas, "you didn't get me dressed yet." He dragged his turtleneck behind him. Ever since he had started going to day care, he insisted on clothes that covered him from head to toe.

"Oh, sweetie," said Billie. "You know we get dressed upstairs."

"Kes told me to go down."

"Oh, jerking off again, is he? All right, come here then."

"What do you mean?" I asked, perturbed.

"Nothing. Kes needs his privacy every once in a while, that's all."

I think she said that just to shut me up, because when Kester came downstairs ten minutes later, the first thing he said was where was his Idadidda-dya.

Here's a picture of Ida a week after her homecoming, at her christening, in the white lace dress that Billie, Kes, Carlos, and I all wore before her. Kester has her in his arms; his hair is Brylcreemed to the side, and he's so proud he doesn't know where to look. Billie is standing next to him, in a demure navy dress that makes her look so sexy you want to lick her like an ice cream pop. Carlos and I both look a little sick, Carlos because he feels sorry for the baby since she'll have to have salt on her lips, I because her name will now be officially pinned on her for all eternity.

I've done my best to make my parents come to their senses about this, but it's hopeless, seeing that my mother thinks it doesn't make any difference whether your name is Margje or Beddy, and as for my father — oh, but he's so proud, he says, of my coming up with the name Ida in the first place! When I think of the priest sprinkling the baptismal water on my little sister's forehead to divulge her name to God, I feel so guilty that I bite my lips with remorse: now Ida will forever be the helpless prey of the evil forces I unleashed months before her birth. There will be a constant stream of fresh demons to torment her. If she dies, it'll be my fault.

My stomach plunges with misery. Please God, strike me with a bolt of lightning. Smite me with an Egyptian plague.

And what do you know, at that very moment a brilliant light flashes twice inside the dusky church. Spooked, I clench my eyes shut.

It's my father's camera. There he is, in a pew over to the side, trying to get all of us into the shot. As he lowers his camera, I see that his eyes are soft and wet.

I once told Billie that in China, his name would be Flashy Flits. Billie responded, snorting with glee, that those dumb slit-eyes over there went around upside down all day, no wonder they always got everything back to front. Anyhow, she wasn't putting up with it anymore, that old stick-in-the-mud expecting her to be home by ten-thirty every night. My mother overheard this exchange, but she didn't get mad at us. All she said was, "Never forget that nobody loves you as much as your father does."

In the photo of Ida's christening, most of the light is focused on Mama's face; it creates sparks in the frizzy ends of her hair, as if she had a halo. She is staring straight ahead, lost in thought. What we don't yet know, as this picture is being taken, is that she has just decided to cut back on her work hours. So many precious weeks have already been wasted that she wants to make up for lost time with Ida. Especially since it's obvious, no matter what the doctors might say, that this baby needs extra attention, after all she's been through —

major surgery to start with, then day after day plugged into all those tubes, and now that poor little head that just doesn't look right.

Margje has always thought of herself as an easygoing mother, not one to fuss. She believes that things will always take their natural course; she trusts in the astonishing resilience of young children. Nor is it in her nature to make a mountain out of a molehill. All of which goes to show there must be something to it, this nagging sense of dread she feels about Ida.

It is so quiet in the church that you can hear the doves cooing outside. A smell of stale incense hovers in the air beneath the vaulted roof. The old priest is mumbling in a monotone. But her children are following the proceedings with rapt attention. Only Ellen is looking away. Her bowed head, with its straight hair hanging down, proclaims rebellion. The first signs of adolescent moodiness. Blink three times and they're ready to go off on their own. Which is just one more good reason not to miss even a second's worth with Ida. She hears her husband's camera click and glances at him. His eyes flicker from her to the children and back again. She knows what he's thinking: You and I, and these our offspring. By God, Margje, this really is ours, this delicious bunch of little monkeys, and this moment too. Suddenly she wants him so badly it makes her blush.

Time and again, he always finds a way to win her over. She used to think that marriage was some sort of status quo, that mutual love and appreciation were a given. In reality, however, there are moments when the very way he clears his throat could be grounds for divorce. Watching him endlessly licking his index finger while thumbing through a clippings file is enough to make your head spin with murderous fantasies. His silences, the ties he selects, the way he answers the phone, his hemming and hawing, his infinite patience, the way his hand brings a spoonful of pudding to his mouth, the very fact of his existence, the fact that he dares even to appear in your presence . . . Get lost, for Christ's sake, go to South America or to Lapland, and don't bother ever coming back.

It would have been ten times worse, Margje thinks, her nipples tingling and her vaginal muscles clenching with desire, with anyone else. She thinks: We really don't make such a bad pair, and she smiles at him.

Ida gives a little yelp. Kester bends over

her, making shushing noises, and gives her his little finger to suck. But Margje's placid mood has already been vaporized, driven out by the jitters. Ida should have had her next feeding by now. Without a moment's hesitation, she snatches her daughter out of Kester's arms and marches out of the church.

It has begun to rain. With the baby in her arms she rushes to the taxi stand at the corner. She can hear her husband calling after her. She gets in and gives the driver her address, brusquely rocking Ida from side to side. We'll be home in no time, little one. The infant is practically blue in the face with hunger, the eyes flat and dull. She smells funny, as if some stranger had pooped in her diaper. A cold fear wraps itself around Margje's heart. She takes Ida's little face in her hands and tries pushing it into the right shape. Don't cry. If you cry, the cab driver will throw you out of the window. His neck is short, thick: that's how you can tell they are child haters.

"Just stop here," she barks.

"Change your mind, lady?"

Without answering she hands him the amount indicated on the meter. She gets out, clutching her whimpering daughter to her chest. That was a close one. But now she'll have to shake him off somehow. She heads in the wrong direction on purpose, in the teeming rain. Suddenly she darts into a side street. A hasty glance over her shoulder reveals she's managed to lose the taxi. Now she can breathe freely again.

It's only when, twenty minutes later, drenched to the skin, she is standing on the front steps of her house, the baby howling in her arms, that the awful truth hits her: the driver knows where she lives — she gave him her address! She'll have to hide Ida. In the kitchen she rips off the dripping-wet christening gown and bundles the baby up in a warm towel. Mama knows a safe hiding place for you. In the suspension file, under M for Manhattan, nobody'll ever come looking for you there. We'll just push the drawer in and no one will be any the wiser, nobody will figure out you're in there, little girl of mine with those gorgeous eyes of yours.

"Mama!" says Ellen, who's suddenly standing in the middle of the kitchen, white-faced. "Where've you been? And why didn't you wait for us at the church?"

Margje stares at her daughter in bewilderment. Then she feels a gush of relief: it's not just up to her now. Ellen is so clever, she'll think of something. "Heavens,

Ellen," she says, rubbing Ida's little back, "you can't imagine how worried I've been."

"What about us?" says her daughter indignantly. "Everyone's been looking for you!" She walks to the cupboard and opens it.

"No chips," Margje says automatically.

"You *never* let me have *anything!*"

"You can have a carrot, or an apple. And please throw these wet things in the hamper for me. Oh, and bring me a clean diaper while you're at it."

Ellen pulls a disgusted face. "You're not going to change her here on the kitchen table, are you? That's where we're having our lunch. That's *so* unhygienic, Mama!"

"You're quite right," says Margje with a sigh, "but wipe that sulk off your face, please, Ellen." With Ida firmly clamped under her arm, she extracts the baby's bottle from the refrigerator. There's endive in there, and some leftover noodles from yesterday. Impatiently she pushes the wet hair back off her forehead with her wrist. Let's hope Billie hasn't forgotten to stop at the butcher's.

Marti, and Sjaak my group leader too, thought it would be best if I went to a different school. Otherwise people would only keep asking me painful questions. I really didn't have any idea what they were talking about, but I didn't mind anyway.

My new school was much closer to the Unicorn, and nobody there had a clue that I'd ever sprained my ankle on a stupid school outing. I ran through the long corridors with my arms spread wide, in a wicked imitation of a dive-bomber. Once or twice, when I'd been rat-tat-tat-ing a bit too wildly, I was called in to see the headmaster. He was very old and had his secretary bring us tea I didn't like the taste of, in fine china cups, with a cookie on the side. On his desk was a plaster bust of Pallas Athena, who stared at me dispassionately with her bulging blank eyes.

Once, he told me that Rotterdam was razed to the ground during the Second World War. He went on about the people in the bomb shelters, and the air-raid sirens. He let me leaf through a whole volume of old black-and-white photos of the bombings. He said that he had been in hiding for over a year and had been very scared.

When I closed the book, abashed, he looked at me, considering. "Do you know how to whistle?"

I nodded.

"Let's hear it then."

I licked my lips and puckered them. Shyly, I whistled: do-re-mi.

"Perfect! Well now, may I suggest that henceforth you try imitating a blackbird instead of a bomber?" Gravely he spread his arms, pretending to fly.

I blushed. "I couldn't. Blackbirds know at least fourteen different melodies!"

"Then you'll just have to practice." He got to his feet to indicate the interview was over. "There are so many things that are worthwhile in life, Ellen. You'll just have to start learning to take pleasure in things again, in what's beautiful, what's right."

From that time on I whistled till I was blue in the face to please him. Oh man, if only they'd given me grades for whistling! When I got my first report card that Christmas, I was at the very bottom of my class. I was having a hard time keeping all those ancient monarchies and battles straight — it was as if my brain was working only in low gear these days — and then there were all the stories about Jason and the Argonauts, and Orpheus who went to look up Eurydice in the underworld. Sometimes I just couldn't tell the difference between what was real and what was made up.

Gerda and Marlies, my roommates, tried to cheer me up about it. Their report cards were even more dismal than mine, they said. They had some hash, and we decided we'd bake hash cookies, to put us in a better mood.

It was the first Saturday of the Christmas vacation. The smell of gingerbread permeated the Unicorn. There was a tree in the living room; the doorposts were decked with holly.

The kitchen radio was blasting out the Top Forty. We poured flour, sugar, and eggs into a bowl; Marlies sprinkled the contents of a little bag of dope into it; and Gerda, snorting with laughter, began stirring. Not to be outdone in the delinquency stakes, I trotted to the living room to see if there were any unguarded packs of cigarettes lying around. And who should I find in there, seated on the sofa, but my little brother Carlos, with Sjaak and Marti, facing a couple of complete strangers! I was nailed to the threshold. The roots of my hair suddenly started to ache.

Sjaak cleared his throat. He said, "This is our Ellen." He waved me over. "Come and shake hands, then."

"Hello, Ellen," said the lady. She had a soft voice, a sad face, and a bun which had

130

strands of graying hair escaping from it.

"Kamphuis," the man introduced himself, sizing me up warily. His tie was on crooked, a wide one, green and blue.

Marti nodded at me encouragingly.

After a moment's hesitation the woman went on, "We thought your brother might like to come to the zoo with us this afternoon."

I was floored. "But — the polar bears always make you cry, and the parrots give you the creeps," I reminded him.

Everyone looked at Carlos, who was blinking rapidly.

"What!" exclaimed Sjaak. "Don't you like elephants either?"

Carlos shook his bowed head.

"Nor monkeys?"

"No," whispered my little brother. He stuck his thumb in his mouth.

"Well done, Ellen," Marti said curtly.

There was a tense silence. Then I offered, "He does like the miniature cities and trains at Madurodam, or the playground, and eating pancakes." I hardly knew myself why I was being so helpful. I wasn't much in the mood for the brownies anymore, and I went to my room, where I sat dejectedly slumped on my quilted bedspread until Marti knocked on the door.

She came in and sat down on the edge of the bed uninvited, resting her hand on my knee. She said that we shouldn't let this opportunity for my brother pass us by, that it was a godsend that these people who wanted to take care of him had come forward. Carlos, she said, had tons of plastic surgery ahead of him; every time he grew a little bigger, he'd have to have another operation. And then who'd pay the hospital bills, and hug him tight when he was scared or in pain? Truly, if everything went ahead as planned and Carlos was indeed chosen by that couple, he'd be a lucky little boy.

"Well, I'm certainly not going with those people."

"No, that was never the intention."

For a brief moment I felt relief. Then I burst out, "But you can't go and give Carlos away, just like that! He isn't yours!"

"He can make up his own mind."

"He belongs with *me!*" My head was practically exploding with dismay. "Without me he'll be an orphan!"

"My dear." She smoothed her skirt. "He already *is* one." She stole a sideways look at me, and waited. Then she sighed and said, "He's not doing at all well, can't you see that for yourself? He needs special

132

care. He refuses to speak, and —"

"So? Is that a reason to do away with him?"

My heart was hammering in my chest. I jumped up wildly and ran into the living room, where Sjaak was gathering up coffee cups. Bowling him aside, I sprinted out of the bungalow. "Carlos," I yelled, beneath the bare trees. "Carlos, come back!"

A few boys from the Rainbow were playing hockey out there, but apart from that the place was deserted.

Just as I started to pick up speed, Sjaak tackled me from behind. "Whoa, just a minute there."

"You dirty traitor!" I screamed, hammering on his chest with both fists. "My brother doesn't belong to you!"

"Oh, come here, girl." He had me pinned in a hold, pressed tight against him. As I struggled, I could smell his sweat, a warm, suffocating smell, and suddenly it felt as if a trapdoor were opening under my feet. I was tumbling head over heels into a dark tunnel, where startling images came at me in short bursts of light, the way they do in the haunted house at the carnival: a discarded pair of boy's socks on the floor under a bed, a sign spelling out "NO ENTRY TO UNAUTHORIZED PERSONS" in cockeyed lettering, a bicycle bell that had been pried to pieces. Somewhere in a dark corner, a boy sat playing a sad tune on a musical saw. When he looked up for a moment, smiling at me guiltily as if I'd caught him in the act, I could see the blackheads on his nose, but the next instant he had vanished like smoke. As I fumbled around blindly in the dark, I was hit with a feeling of such homesickness — deeper and wider than the ocean, a bottomless pit — that my knees began knocking with terror. And then suddenly he popped up again, right in front of me, on his bicycle, with two fat saddlebags bulging with packages. Running after him, I jumped onto his rear carrier. I flung my arms around his waist and pressed my face into the folds of his T-shirt, making him swerve, so that he shouted over his shoulder, "Can't you take your own bike, Ellen? Ellen?"

"Ellen!" Sjaak was shaking me. "Ellen, come on, snap out of it!" Looming up behind him out of the dingy wintery light, I could make out a tangle of boys. I heard the dull whack of their hockey sticks against the ball, like the snap of breaking bones. There was snow in the air, and the wind was bitterly cold.

I sank against Sjaak in a daze. How did

134

they *do* that? Did they use some kind of transmitter or something, way out on some far-off planet? Could they simply implant something like that into your head, a boy with a musical saw, and then have him swim via the bloodstream to your heart and worm his way inside, filling you with such desperate longing that it gave you the shakes? Again I could see him before me, so familiar and yet so desperately out of my reach. And in that instant, I knew that he was dead.

"What would you say to a nice hot mug of cocoa?" Sjaak's nose had turned red from the cold.

How, I wondered in alarm, does one get to know the things one knows? "What happens to dead people?" I asked shrilly.

Sjaak looked at me closely. "Oh, sweetheart, well, I suppose . . . I think, yes, I think they live on inside us. As long as we don't forget them, they're always with us."

"Oh," I said.

He led me indoors and told me I could help myself to one of the chocolate ornaments off the tree while he prepared the cocoa in the kitchen.

I took down a little chocolate wreath with white dots that crunched between my teeth. Now that I knew he was there, I could clearly feel the boy with the saw sitting inside my heart, in the lower left-hand ventricle. He had probably always been there, neglected and forgotten, like a little mole on my arm, a pebble in my sock, a name on the tip of my tongue. I hugged myself, rocking from side to side.

*Tell me, stranger, do you enjoy being in there?*

*Well, to be quite frank with you, Ellen, I'm loving every minute of it.*

A hoarse voice, a crooked grin, a monster zit on his cheek, greasy fingers. *Carlos, go downstairs now, man, go on. I need a little privacy.*

"Kester," I whispered.

"Ellen," he answered softly. "I thought you'd forgotten me."

"And me," said Billie. She was standing next to him, with drooping shoulders, her eyelids swollen and red.

Slowly they walked up to me, their faces taut with the effort not to cry. Kester who could swim underwater for a minute and a half and who was saving up for a motorcycle that he was going to soup up; Billie who waxed her legs and who slept with the nail of her pinky poking into her cheek because she wanted to have a dimple there. All my life, not a minute had gone by that hadn't involved their dreams, their projects, and their presence, intrusive and familiar; unavoidable, inescapable. They were older than my oldest self; they were an inextricable part of me.

"How *could* you have left us to rot like that?" seethed Billie.

Bewildered, I tried to find the words that would make everything OK again. Billie, we've got some hash brownies. Want my piece?

Kester cuffed his fingers around my wrist. The set of screwdrivers hanging from his belt clashed and jangled. "Where's Charlie?" he rasped.

"He's gone to Madurodam."

"But Madurodam's closed in the winter."

Startled, I looked down at the ground.

"You'd better start looking after him a little better, or you'll lose him. You don't pay enough attention to him."

"Just as you ditched us back there," said Billie.

When I realized what she meant, I gasped. "But what else could I have done! Carlos was the only one I could still . . ."

"What about us, then?" asked Billie, taking my hand. Her lashes were caked with mascara. "If you had to choose all over again, wouldn't you have tried to —"

"There wasn't any choice!"

"Oh come on!" Billie was now weeping openly. "Don't you love me, then?"

Kester pulled at my arm. "Hey, you're my little sister, aren't you?"

"Ellen!" Billie tugged at my hand. "Who was it who taught you how to French-kiss!"

"Ellen!" said Kester. "If it hadn't been for me you'd still be stuck in that roof gutter blubbering because you didn't have the guts to climb down!"

"Ellen!" said Billie. "Didn't I always share everything with you? Even my white lipstick!"

"Ellen!" said Kester. "I always let you stick the stamps on the packages because you liked the taste of the glue. And whenever you had a flat tire, I always let you ride up front, on my handlebars."

"Ellen!" said Billie. "Doesn't any of this *mean* anything to you? Don't you ever think of anybody but yourself?"

Kester said, "And could you please explain to us why you're still alive and we're not?"

Billie said, "We know you always felt superior, getting those high grades all the time, and being such a know-it-all about grammar and stuff."

Kester said, "So are you happy now, without us?"

"Leave me alone," I stammered, slinging my arms protectively over my head.

"No way," Billie taunted. "You're never going to sleep another night without us from now on, I promise you."

"You'll never get rid of us again," said Kester.

One by one I spat out the horrifying words: "But you guys . . . are . . . dead."

"Well, OK, but now that you remember us again . . ." began Kes.

". . . we'll live on inside you," Billie decided. She frowned. "So, did you finally get your period?"

Kester said, "Gross."

Billie said, *You don't have to love me, Rhett. Just kiss me.*

*"Oh, Scarlett,"* said Kes. *"Don't get killed."*

Billie's black hair swinging like a pennant, and Kester's bony arms spread wide for a hug. Then they faded away again. Only Billie's wide mouth floated in the air for an instant, like the Cheshire cat in *Alice in Wonderland.* "Just make sure nothing happens to Carlos. Or we'll come and fetch him ourselves."

I sat doubled over on the sofa in the Unicorn when Sjaak came in with our cocoa.

"Ellen?" said Marti. She was standing next to Sjaak with an expectant look on her face.

I braced myself with whatever strength I had left. "Yes?"

"Sjaak got the impression . . ." She flashed me a thin-lipped smile. I had to remind myself I couldn't trust her. "Sjaak thought you might have been thinking of your parents just now."

"No I wasn't."

"We can understand that you'd sooner forget them, but you can't go on like this for the rest of your life. We would so like to help you to . . ."

I started picking at the hem of my sweater. "When's Carlos coming home?"

"At six. But, Ellen . . ."

I wasn't listening. I gulped down my cocoa. "I still have a book to read for my research project," I informed them.

In Carlos's room I grabbed a pair of pants, a sweatshirt, and a handful of socks from his closet and stuffed them into my swimming bag along with his chewed-up teddy bear. Then I sat down at the desk in my own room and began reading about

King Xerxes of Persia, who marched on Greece in 481 B.C. with a huge host. By a quarter to six the letters were doing jumping-jacks all over the page. I was underlining words at random with my ruler and a red pen. At ten past six Carlos stormed in, eyes bright with excitement, a new Matchbox toy clutched in his little fist. For me there was a candy cane in a crinkly wrapper with little hearts on it. He had already sucked on it himself.

"I've been on a merry-go-round," he began ecstatically. "And we —"

"No, keep your coat on. We're going out for a bit too, just the two of us this time."

He flopped onto my bed. "But I want to play with my new car."

"Shut up." I threw my jacket on, patted my pocket to make sure I had my wallet with my spending money, slung the bag over my shoulder, and pushed my little brother out into the hall. Hurry up. Sjaak would be setting the table for supper, and Marti was probably in her office, talking things over with that necktie and that hair-bun who wanted to take Carlos home with them.

Outside it was pitch-dark. Snow was coming down in large, wet, loose flakes. I didn't dare take the bus in case the driver remembered us later. We had to walk down the whole length of the highway. My sneakers were sopping wet in no time. Carlos whined all the way. Where are we going? Why do we have to walk so far? They were all so convinced he never said a word, and meanwhile he was driving me nuts with his big mouth!

We passed large old houses with bright Christmas wreaths on their front doors and trees festooned with little lights in their yards. Tomorrow was Christmas Day.

Once in a while a car would come by and I'd quickly yank Carlos back into the hedge. I promised him a fire engine and real rubber boots for his bear. I told him about Hannibal and his elephants in the Alps. Talk about hardships . . . !

At last we came to an area where the houses were closer together. My feet were so cold that they ached, and every time I stopped to fasten Carlos's hood more tightly, I thought my shoes would freeze to the ground. In the distance, a church bell rang seven times. That must be St. Bavo's. If it was open, we'd be able to warm our hands at the candles on the Holy Virgin's altar.

The church we finally reached was small and dark, and the square it stood on didn't look right, either. Carlos sat down on the curb. I promised him French fries. Nobody could accuse me of not looking after him well. If it hadn't been for him, I'd be eating a hash brownie now, sitting by the fire with Marlies and Gerda. I tugged on his arm to haul him to his feet.

We wandered through quiet streets that were all equally unfamiliar to me. The sidewalks were so slippery you could break your neck. At every corner, I would tell Carlos we were nearly there. My tongue kept getting stuck between my chattering teeth. Carlos slipped and fell down; he started bawling, in long drawn-out gasps. His pants were all wet and dirty from his fall. My fingers rigid with cold, I unbuttoned his fly in a doorway and pulled his pants down. His knees were blue; I planted a loud smacking kiss on each one, then bundled him as quickly as I could into the dry pair from my swim bag. I pulled the extra socks I'd brought over his hands as mittens, stuffing them up his sleeves as far as they would go. "And now, let's sing," I said. "Come on. *Left, right. Left, right. I left because I couldn't do right, I couldn't do right so I left.*"

At a big intersection, I spotted neon signs shimmering in the distance. We trudged toward them. A drafty shopping mall, a closed supermarket, an auto parts store, a tile shop. I let Carlos pick out a tile. Surely we must be getting close to the center of town now.

The streetlights shone weakly. Our breath puffed out like smoke. The bag containing Carlos's wet pants kept growing heavier on my shoulder. I had to drag my brother along by the arm. My teeth were locked together.

We went down into a pedestrian underpass. Despite the cold, it stank of pee, and the arches were covered in lurid graffiti. Coming up on the other side, I spotted a railway siding. I began pushing my brother along the tracks. His breath was coming out in ragged gasps.

Side by side we plodded along the tracks. It was less slippery if you stepped on the gravel between the ties. We were making good headway.

My shoes were squelching. My eyes darted from side to side, on the lookout for familiar landmarks.

Carlos stopped, yammering that he refused to go any farther. I hoisted him onto my back; at every step his heels banged into my sides. Suddenly a train loomed up ahead of us and I dived sideways, flattening myself against the bank. The rattling cars flashed by, stirring up such a blast of wind that my hair whipped against my cheeks. When I finally scrambled back to my feet, I left my swimming bag where it lay on the gravel. I was too tired to bend over and pick it up.

I trudged on and on. The snow crunched softly beneath my soles. My brother hung on my back like a sack of coal, his arms wrapped so tightly around my neck I nearly choked. But I would get him to safety, on that he could rely. Just let anybody, alive or dead, try to take him away from me.

Finally the lights of a railway station came into sight, twinkling in the distance. When, fifteen minutes later, we staggered up under the cement awning and I was able to read the signs on the platform, the shock made my head reel. We hadn't been walking toward the center of Haarlem at all, we had been heading in the opposite direction: this was Overveen Station. There was no railway buffet here where I could buy fries for Carlos: it was one of those dumb old local stops where the ticket office closes early and a train comes chugging by just once every half-hour.

We sat on the deserted platform for an

eternity, behind a billboard that offered some shelter from the wind. Carlos wanted his teddy, and as I wasn't about to tell him that I had left it on the tracks, I launched into a complicated story that I had a hard time bringing to a happy ending. I urgently needed to pee, but everything was locked. On a window a piece of paper was posted. It said that since it was Christmas the schedule was changed and there would be no more trains after ten-thirty.

Wheedling didn't work anymore. I had to threaten Carlos with a good spanking to get him moving again.

We walked through the deserted village until we saw a road sign pointing to Haarlem. My feet shuffled forward on automatic pilot. It felt as though I had been dragging my little brother through this freezing night my entire life, while our destination kept moving further out of reach. We crossed the Western Ring Road. The entire Zijlweg lay ahead of us. At the Leiden canal we had to battle the wind, which was blowing in our faces. When I went to the prep school, I used to come this way every day on my bike; just the idea that I was on familiar ground inspired me with renewed resolve. In the distance, the bells were ringing for midnight mass.

Carlos tripped and fell, and I had to carry him piggyback again. He had lost one of his improvised mittens. I could feel his snot trickling down my neck. At the corner of the Kampersingel canal I almost gave up. Come on, it's not far now. Number 23. Or was it 32? I couldn't remember the street number I had printed on the Christmas card that I'd mailed earlier in the week. I hadn't been able to find a card with a blackbird on it, so I had sent him one of a robin hopping through the snow with clever beady eyes. I knew the headmaster would appreciate it just the same.

There was no light on at number 32. There was no name on the door either. I staggered on, to the odd numbers across the bridge on the other side of the canal. The metal railing was so cold that my hand stuck to it. I counted the houses. Number 23 looked dark too. I just didn't know anymore. I stood on the steps, Carlos hanging on my back, in the silentest night of the year, crushed by the realization that there was really no one left in the whole world who could help me.

I let Carlos slide down off my back and sagged against the windowsill. Suddenly I noticed a crack of light between the drawn curtains. Trembling, I stretched my hand toward the bell and pushed it.

After a few moments the light in the hall flicked on. The door opened. I hardly recognized him at first, without his reading glasses and in a funny red sweater jacket I had never seen him wear at school. As I opened my mouth to say something, my lower lip split open; besides blood I also could suddenly taste salty tears in my mouth. I pushed Carlos out in front of me like a shield. "This is my little brother," I blurted out. "Could he hide here with you for a while?"

Now that the nights are getting longer, I often work in the yard until the last bit of light is gone. Slash and prune, that's my motto. You start with a timid snip here, a light trim there, but you end up with the scythe, the pickax, and the grim determination to show nature who's boss. What you want is to get down to the bare bones, create order out of chaos. Chop until you drop. Out with those towering nettles and ferns, and the ivy that's running amok.

Sometimes Bas will come over on his bike after work with a few seedlings, an extra bag of lime for the grass, a roll of chicken wire. He inspects my progress, offers advice, praises my ingenuity. That gate over there — what a perfect solution. What a good job you've done of assembling that pergola. I shrug my shoulders. I'm not afraid of handling tools. After all, I have Kes telling me exactly what to do.

In the late afternoon sun, Bas and I drink a cup of tea on the mossy terrace and nibble on the first strawberries of the season. I never ask him to come inside, and he doesn't push it, either. We don't say much; certainly we say nothing about the year when I was twelve and he was twenty-four. It's a deliberate silence that, strangely enough, seems perfectly natural. What can we be expected to say, after all, about something which is, by definition, unspeakable? Having mutely agreed on that point, we are simply two old acquaintances contentedly involved in a common project. I catch myself looking forward to his company. Bas doesn't own a boat, or his own Web page, or a Rolex. Not even a decent pair of sunglasses.

He lives in the city, in an apartment, he tells me, over a little shop selling Spanish antiques that attracts few browsers. He has planted a garden on the roof. You should see my clematis: it's grown right over to the building across the alley. Oh, and then I have that white riverbed gravel for edging. You could use some of that here. He waves, offhandedly, at the long drive. I can picture him puttering about on his little roof, a giant among his six pots of geraniums and three pots of fuchsias, cheerfully whistling through his teeth. He often talks to himself, the way people who live alone do. "OK, we'll tackle this here first," he'll say out loud, to spur himself on, "that way we'll have a clearer view." "Perfect!" "Well, look what we've got here." "Ah, *that's* better."

Come on, Bas, what's keeping you tonight? That old honeysuckle needs to come out; I have my heart set on getting it done. Know what? I'll just start on it myself. The sweat is soon dripping into my eyes, my shirt clinging to my back. After wrestling with the overgrown vine for a good fifteen minutes, I hear his bicycle bell.

Not bothering with a hello, he walks over, watches for a moment, then takes the saw out of my hand, waves me aside, and dispatches the creaking bush in no time flat. Well, no wonder, with all the groundwork I'd already done for him. Then he

150

picks up a spade and begins hacking at the roots. His stringy ponytail sticks to his neck.

I bundle up the debris and gleefully dump it in the center of the path. Nothing can spoil my mood now.

"So when are you going to start planting your seeds?" he asks over his shoulder.

"Oh, I don't know, when there's a full moon or something."

"It's supposed to rain tonight. And your flower beds are ready for it."

But I'm not. I'm still fixated on hacking and pruning. The tender nursing of germinating green can wait. "Do you want something to drink?" I ask, to change the subject.

"I'll just move those hollyhocks first. They don't get enough sunlight over here."

"They will if I get rid of that hedge."

"You might as well pour cement everywhere," he snaps testily. Using the shovel as a crowbar, he pries the roots out of the ground effortlessly. It's only when I see Bas at work that I truly understand all the ways in which Prozac has saved his life. Someone with his strength can't afford any irrational outbursts. He flings the clump into the wheelbarrow and turns his large face toward me. It is crumpled with rage.

Involuntarily I take a step backward.

"Nature, Ellen, living things," he says, waving his arm at the old oaks with their naked crowns and the marsh marigolds in the scummy pond. "Can't you show it some fucking respect?"

"But you always say yourself you can never be too ruthless when you're pruning."

"And, besides," he seethes, pointing at my midriff, "I shouldn't think it's all that sensible, to slave your guts out like this in your condition."

"My condition!" Suddenly we're standing there snarling at each other like pit bulls. "My condition is *my* business!"

"You mean I'm supposed to pretend I can't see you're expecting?"

"Now *you* listen to *me*." But that's all I can manage. Livid with rage I grab the wheelbarrow and tip it over onto the compost heap. Good Lord, I'm not about to let some salesclerk from the garden center tell me off! Living nature, my foot! I tip the wheelbarrow over savagely. Stomp back. Bark, in a loud, icy voice, "Bas!"

"Watering can," he snaps back at me. He has already dug the holes for the hollyhocks.

I stomp stiffly to the tap, fill the zinc watering can, lug it to the flower bed, dump its contents.

Deftly he tamps down the wet earth around the plants. Then he growls, scowling, "Doesn't that poor child have a father?"

"Buzz off," I answer calmly.

He looks at me incredulously. His eyebrows are grown together above his eyes, the deep groove at the root of his nose is dirty, the pores are visible, his hair is limp with grease. A candidate for the Lonely Hearts Club if there ever was one. Which might explain why he shows up at my place practically every day.

He hauls himself to his feet. "You can't order me around. I'm not going."

"Well!" I say. I'm shaking. "That really is the fucking limit."

"Oh, you needn't try that princess-and-the-pea routine on me. Night after night, there's nobody else that shows up to give you a hand, is there!"

"Which doesn't alter the fact that this is *my* property and I am entitled to refuse you access."

"*Entitled to refuse you access*," he laughs, snorting. "You always *were* full of shit."

"I don't need anybody," I say wildly.

He cranes his neck forward and mows

153

his arms through the air as if clearing a space in order to fire his words at me. "What the hell are you trying to prove, Ellen? That a child is better off having as few parents as possible?" Then he wipes his hands on his pants and stomps out of the garden through the new gate.

I dig my nails into my palms. Where were we? Pull down the grapevine from the shed, that was another thing I was going to get to tonight. I'll start on it in a minute. Tomorrow I'll rent a trailer for the car to get rid of the debris. They already know me at the town dump. The guard waves at me from his little office when he sees me at the gate. As long as he doesn't get it into his head that my condition is any of his business, either. "Don't you have a husband, lady, who can do the heavy work?"

That reminds me, suddenly, of Thijs. Ever since that one time he came here to drop off that notice, I haven't heard a word from him. I realize I'm exhausted. I collect the gardening tools and drag them into the shed. In the kitchen I open a bottle of mineral water and guzzle it down, standing at the sink.

One of my shrinks, the last one, I believe, used to say that I am bent on sabotaging my own happiness. I don't know which I find more irritating: the claptrap litany of clichés, or the fact that the clichés usually turn out to be correct. I'll probably never hear from Thijs again. I think I did him a great service by having him find me accidentally standing at my door with Bas. It must finally have dawned on him: Ellen is a hopeless case. And Bas, in his own way, is welcome to the same conclusion.

It is still early, but I decide to take myself to bed. It's the right thing to do, for a mother with child.

To Thijs's disappointment, I didn't want to have kids, ever. So now you see: a person can change her mind, although I can't pretend, either, that getting pregnant was in any way a conscious decision. Was it simply that my so-called biological clock decided to take affairs into its own little hands as soon as my fortieth birthday loomed on the horizon? You hear that this sort of thing does happen. Smothered instincts have been known to burst forth from where they've lain buried just before the final bell. Or is it simply that I feel I have a certain responsibility: If I don't come through, where will the next generation of Van Bemmels come from?

There is still Carlos of course, but, by

the same token, not really: he stopped being my brother twenty-five years ago, when he turned into Michael Kamphuis, shortly after that infamous Christmas Eve.

We had sat huddled together on my headmaster's sofa for hours, wrapped in blankets, a hot-water bottle resting on our feet and cups of hot milk in our hands. It astonished me that someone who had a bust of Pallas Athena on his desk could be married to someone so old and so ugly. Also, she couldn't seem to stop shaking. Begrudgingly, she offered us each a sliver of Christmas cake with almond filling and the skimpiest scrape of butter on it. I was glad when she went to bed, mumbling nervously to herself.

Next to me, Carlos was already asleep, half keeled over on his side.

The headmaster and I played chess by the light of the floorlamp, the chessboard balanced on a footstool between us. He wasn't familiar with the Scholar's Mate, so I won the first round. We began lining up the pieces for another game.

"My wife has Parkinson's disease," he said. "So it's impossible for us to look after your little brother, Ellen. You have to understand that."

I was white. I opened with a pawn.

"By the way, who taught you to play chess so well?"

"My father," I answered automatically.

"Well, he sure knew what he was doing."

Thunder roared inside my ears. "Dad!" I exclaimed, totally bewildered. It felt as if an electric current were zapping through me from the top of my head to the tip of my toes.

"You must be having a very hard time coming to terms with what happened," the headmaster said. "And it is possible you may never come to grips with it entirely. But there is one thing I can swear to you, cross my heart. You will learn to cope one day, believe me. Even if you can't imagine ever doing so right now."

I stared at the chessboard, which was made of wood, not plywood, speckled with age, like ours. My father used to say that those marks were made by the sweat of his brow. "You never make it easy for me," he'd sigh, and then he'd wink at me over the rim of his glasses.

"I don't suppose it's much of a consolation, is it?" Frowning, the headmaster inched his knight forward, then took it back again. His fingers waved indecisively over the board, and the light from the lamp cast heavy shadows over his face.

"May I sit on your lap?" I blurted out.

"All right, come here, my girl." He spread his arms.

Trying to get to my feet, I got all tangled up in my blanket and almost fell off the sofa. He drew me onto his knee. I curled up in a ball and pressed my head into his chest. I could hear his heartbeat, his heart that said, You are fine, Ellen, just the way you are.

After a little while I stuck my thumb in my mouth.

Then I felt his breath on my ear. "Ellen? In a little while, when you're asleep, I'll call the Home, and tell them you're here. Otherwise they won't get a wink of sleep tonight. Is that all right with you?"

Sleepily I felt around for Carlos's hand. "Sorry I lost your bear, Charlie," I muttered.

Ten days later my brother decamped to the Kamphuis family. It was just a trial visit, they all said, to see if it would work. I marked off every day on my pony calendar. But the days turned into weeks, the ice in the ditches melted, a new orphan moved into the Unicorn, and Carlos never came back to me.

If my brother's adoptive parents had any

sense, they'd have been well advised to avoid telling him much about his origins. All he stood to gain, by knowing who he really was, was the unbearable knowledge that his own parents had murdered his siblings before doing away with themselves.

God Almighty, do I need a drink.

I heave myself out of bed again, even though I've only just gotten in. The dark empty house makes me feel, for a moment, like a tiny pea rattling around helplessly in a great big pod. My renovation plans are going nowhere. I've let the garden take up much too much of my time. While I'm still feeling fit and mobile, I really should do first things first.

In the kitchen I take out the bottle of gin. Now to find the smallest possible glass; otherwise, it will go down too quickly. Whenever I've had a few, I always get the urge to do something rash. Such as going to bed with total strangers and forgetting to take the pill to boot. Still, this pregnancy, though unplanned, is no accident. I have this feeling that all the departed ones in the world got together at some point to cast the die, taking the decision out of my hands unanimously.

I knew it was meant to be when I saw the house advertised. Call it a simple case of seeing the writing on the wall.

I put my hands on my stomach. "Come on, we're going back to bed," I tell Ida-Sophie. At least she hasn't had to hang around and wait for a flat tire on some random Tuesday morning. I've taken some of the uncertainty out of the game: I've given Lady Luck a little push on her behalf.

She is germinating, cell by cell, a mind-boggling process. She grows more real to me every day: a being with little knees and tiny elbows — my daughter. Who will she look like? Will she have an irresistible little mole at the corner of her mouth just like Billie? Will she have my slanty eyebrows?

Never in my life have I wanted anything as badly as this child.

I tidy my glass away. I switch off the light. Suddenly a razor-sharp pain tears at my lower abdomen. It feels as if I'm being ripped open with a knife. I can't move. My fingers are clamped around the back of my chair; I can see my knuckles turning white. And then I feel the blood running down between my legs.

*Part Two*

# Kester, Ellen, and Bas, Thanksgiving, 28 November 1972

Every morning starts with a cup of tea and a piece of toast in bed. Then the venetian blind is raised and the new day leaps into my room like a snarling beast. I wish I could run to the window and fling it open, shouting, "I'm still in here! Wait for me!" But Lucia is already lifting me onto the bedpan, I am given a bowl of warm water to wash myself with, and my wrinkled bedsheets are smoothed flat.

If I feel the need for a clean T-shirt, I have to ask for it more than once. When Lucia first arrived here on such short notice, she had hardly any clothes with her apart from the too-tight pink leggings that she wears day in, day out. My clothes, stacked in neat little piles in Bas's old cupboard, must be making her sweat with envy. It's obvious: her frenzied gestures betray her hostility, which smolders inside those piercing dark eyes. Sometimes I half expect an electric shock from being touched by her. She usually keeps her lips

163

pressed tightly together, to hide the fact she's missing a couple of front teeth.

Lucia is not my nurse by my choosing, or by her own. Fate has saddled us with each other, or, rather, Dr. Bramaan has. Peace has been in short supply in my house ever since. Lucia has three little girls, skittish little things with pale, tense faces, who are easily overexcited. Their squabbles and screams echo loudly through the still sparsely furnished rooms.

If I complain about the noise, their mother just gives a sullen shrug. In her view, there probably exists some sort of hierarchy of suffering, and all I am is someone with a placenta that threatens to become detached. Someone with a good excuse to lie flat on her back for a few months and let someone else wait on her hand and foot. A spoiled, stuck-up bitch in a ridiculously large house. I suspect her of deliberately gouging the paintwork and secretly gloating over every piece of china destroyed by her daughters. But what did I expect? That Lucia and little Samantha, Vanessa, and Rochelle would grovel at my feet in gratitude? They have only Jan Bramaan to thank for this temporary shelter in the Lijsterlaan. And rightly so.

Johnnie Bramaan, says Lucia with obstinate affection, is a prince, the best. You can count on him.

I thought so too when, three weeks ago, he found me lying in a puddle of blood on the kitchen floor in the middle of the night. The ambulance took its time getting there, and he held my hand the whole time. I was in such pain I couldn't speak; I had to signal to him in Morse code with my fingers. The most comforting thing was that he didn't act too concerned. Every time I thought I was going to die, or that Ida-Sophie would come spurting out of me on a tidal wave of blood, I'd see him stifling a yawn. He was a sleepy mass of muscle, fat, and bone, a lifebuoy made of flesh, to which the two of us could cling for dear life.

Two days later he came and visited me in the hospital. We went over all the options. I was still giddy with painkillers, and he had the cunning of a fox. Hospitals weren't set up for the sort of extended bed rest the specialist had prescribed for me. In ten days I would have to go home. Did I have any friends or family members who might come and take care of me? A visiting nurse wasn't the answer: lying flat on your back for twenty-four hours a day required round-the-clock care. Did I have insurance? Or any other means to pay for it?

The habit of a lifetime almost caused me to nod my head yes automatically: the Lijsterlaan rainy-day fund. Except that it didn't exist anymore. My entire nest egg had gone into four impassive walls that couldn't care less about my plight.

"You have a large house," Bramaan remarked, as if he had read my mind.

So we came to an agreement. He would provide the extra mattresses and linens. By the time I was discharged from the hospital, Lucia and her little girls had already made themselves at home. Their noisy presence called attention to the emptiness of the rooms, the hollowness of the corridors. I had my nose painfully rubbed in the fact that none of my elaborate plans had come to fruition yet — which did little to put me in a better mood. Even worse, I thought I recognized Lucia as one of the women who used to give my new designer handbag such hateful looks in Bramaan's waiting room. I'd just as soon have seen her cut out at once.

But fine, there we are: and for the time being neither of us can afford to be choosy. Every time she helps me onto the bedpan before I go to sleep, I can read in her face that she too can think of more agreeable ways of passing the time. The alternative, however, is the overcrowded battered women's shelter in Haarlem, and Lucia has been there often enough. Don't ask me why she keeps going back to her old man. Don't ask me anything. I am a doctor for the dead, not the living, with their fears and pains, their troubles, their hope, and their despair. I don't have any patients who swear they fell down the stairs again or walked into a door. I know nothing of Lucia's problems. I don't want to, either. The thought of her fills me with revulsion: imagine bringing children into this world, as if it were no big deal, and then not having the wherewithal to give them a safe home!

She is standing by my bed, my toothbrush at the ready.

"I don't feel like going to sleep yet," I protest. Suddenly the telephone on the night table starts to ring, and she freezes.

I feel compelled to offer nothing but an extremely reserved "Hello?" when I pick up the phone. Not that I ever answer the phone any other way, actually.

"Ha, Ellen!" Bas responds, equally guarded. His voice over the receiver sounds so familiar, but so strange, too, that

I am for a moment at a loss for words.

"I happened to be riding by your house this afternoon and I noticed you hadn't done anything about the garden in ages." He pauses expectantly. "And so I wondered if there was something wrong?"

Lucia stares at me wide-eyed. She is holding my toothbrush like a spear. I look away. Now that you mention it, Bas, I've been lying here in bed for three weeks because I almost had a miscarriage. But then suppose he asks me how I am managing, all by myself. Or, worse still, suppose he comes over with a bunch of grapes. When Bramaan laid it all out for me, it made perfect sense: any and every contact with the outside world carries a certain measure of risk. Even people with the best of intentions could cause trouble if they recognized Lucia, or, worse, if by some fluke they were friends-of-a-friend of her husband's. In exchange for my care, I gladly gave Jan Bramaan my word that I would not jeopardize her safety or that of her children.

I hear her breathing beside me, in rapid, shallow gasps.

"Ellen, are you there?" asks Bas.

I have the words ready on the tip of my tongue. "I'm sorry I bit your head off, the last time. I meant to call you that same evening. But I almost had a mis . . ." Instead, I say evenly, "I'm afraid you must have the wrong number."

As I hang up the receiver, Lucia's lips part and I can see the gap in her teeth.

"It's OK," I say, collapsing back onto my pillows. "It was for me."

"Are you sure?"

"Yes. Somebody I used to know."

She points at my belly with the toothbrush. "The one who saddled you with that?"

"No one's saddled me with anything."

"Oh, sure, and that's why you're now lying here all by your lonesome." With a scornful scowl she hands me the toothbrush, a glass of water, and a bowl to spit in. I suppose Bramaan must have thought, Ellen van Bemmel doesn't have anyone anyway, not much chance of unexpected visitors or busybodies that like to stick their noses in. And yet there *is* someone out there who is thinking of me, who is concerned about me.

I rinse out my mouth, then turn over onto my side without another word, pulling the covers up to my nose.

"Well, good night then," says Lucia. She takes it upon herself to turn out the light.

Outside I hear a woodpecker hammering away in the dusk of the late-summer evening. He is pecking at the bark of a tree close to my window. Other than that, it is quiet. Even the house is peaceful, for a change.

If Bas knew I was lying here, in the very spot where his desk used to be, if he knew that I am gazing at the same view he enjoyed for years while answering the phone . . . if Bas only knew!

It's too absurd, to allow myself to be bullied by someone like Lucia in my own house. I turn over to pick up the phone, but as I lift the receiver, I hear a busy tone. My jailer must have left the receiver off the hook in another room. Damn her. I should never have let myself get mixed up in this. As Kester likes to say, "Don't get involved with strangers, kiddo. People from different backgrounds are nothing but trouble."

"Such a nuisance," says Billie. "You really can't put yourself in another person's shoes, Ellen, and don't expect her to understand *you*, either."

※　※　※　※　※　※

Every Wednesday at the stroke of midnight, I would wait for Gerda and Marlies

170

by the hollow tree behind the Unicorn. The rotted trunk was where we stashed our supply of hash, in three layers of plastic wrap, as well as the beers we'd smuggled out of the supermarket under piles of toilet paper when we were sent by Sjaak to do the shopping.

I can still see my agitated breath steaming up into the dark night sky. I remember how I used to prick up my ears. The password was Folks Are Just Plain Crazy. Dry leaves rustled under my jittery feet. I couldn't keep them still, because the suspense was killing me: Were they coming, or not? I was always the first one to get there.

But here they were, giggling, with an extra scarf for me, you silly goose, can't you ever dress yourself properly?

The winter Carlos was taken from me, it froze so hard that there were often splinters of ice floating in our beers. In the dark, huddled deep in our coats, we hung around that massive trunk, stamping our feet and clutching our beers with fingers turning blue, discussing our future in stage whispers.

Since we were best friends, I was going to be a fashion model too, just like Gerda and Marlies. As soon as we got the chance, we were going to catch a train to Milan, where we'd take our tops off and install ourselves on some beach somewhere. The rest would take care of itself.

At school, or in bed, thinking about what we'd decided to do would make me go all warm with delight. Suddenly, scoring my arms and legs surreptitiously with a piece of broken glass lost its appeal. I cut myself, Marti said, only because my memory was beginning to return. Memories, she said, sometimes enticed you to do nasty things to yourself, against your better judgment. It was just a matter of being able to keep the upper hand. And the only way to do that was to stand and face the memories head-on, instead of trying to run away.

That was why, a few weeks after Christmas, she made me visit the cemetery, accompanied by Sjaak and herself. Marti held me by the hood of my jacket as we walked through the snowy cemetery, Sjaak striding ahead of us with a bunch of flowers. He was wearing his Palestinian scarf.

At the grave, Marti squatted down and brushed the snow aside with her mittens so that I could read the inscription, which had been deeply chiseled into the rugged stone:

*Frits Gerardus Theodorus van Bemmel*
*Margreet Magdalena van Bemmel-de Groot*
*Sybille Maria van Bemmel*
*Kester Antonius Christiaan van Bemmel*
*Ida Johanna van Bemmel*

My first thought was: It isn't them. Kester Antonius Christiaan couldn't possibly be my brother Kes. But then the enemy, a.k.a. my memory, produced the beloved, familiar faces I missed so much: Kes with his shiny nose, Billie with her long hair braided, my father peering over the top of his reading glasses, his eyes rimmed red with tiredness. I quickly switched my attention to the dates, from which you could tell what age they had all reached. But of course that also told you they were all dead.

Through a haze of tears I began prying the snow out of the letter O of Kester's Antonius. Perhaps that was the way the dead addressed each other — formally, by their full names. If that was the case, I had better follow suit from now on, or they might not hear me.

Sjaak handed me the flowers, so I could put them down on the grave. Dark red roses, with lovely long stems. If I left them in the snow, they'd die. I really didn't see

173

the point. They belonged in a vase.

"Are you all right, Ellen?" Marti asked softly, behind me.

If you looked closely, you could see that the stone was shaped like a heart, an ice-cold heart of stone that would outlive everyone without beating even once. It would still be there when everyone underneath it was long forgotten. In time, slowly but inexorably, even the names of my whole family would be eroded away, until all that was left was the weathered surface.

I wiped my nose on my sleeve. Where did you go once your name was erased? How would anyone be able to get in touch with you then?

With a shock, I suddenly noticed that room had been left on the headstone for Carlos and me. The roses slipped out of my hand and spilled onto the snow like drops of blood. I spun around on my heels and, without thinking, started running.

The road was hard and silent. The only thing I could hear was my own breathing. The bald trees along the road danced before my eyes.

Marlies's parents had died in a traffic accident. Gerda's parents had both fallen ill and died within months of each other when she was a little girl. Unlike their parents, mine hadn't deserted me by accident. For me it had been quite the other way around. The blank space on the headstone made me realize that they had meant me to end up under that heart of stone as well, together with them.

I had no right to be alive. Apparently I never had that right; or Mama and Dad would have made other plans for me. They had decided I was better off dead, and your own parents know what's best for you. Somewhere deep in the center of the earth, they were tormenting themselves over me now, their obstinate, pigheaded daughter. I must be such a disappointment to them.

I raced back to the Unicorn, running all the way until my lungs were about ready to explode.

Gerda and Marlies were making a snowman in front of our bungalow. They were gleefully rolling one large snowball on top of another, as if all the snow in the world belonged to them by right; as if it had been snowing from here to the North Pole solely for their benefit. "Want to join us?" cried Marlies.

I shook my head.

In my room I stretched out on the bedspread that wasn't really mine and thought about Milan, about the future that now didn't seem to be mine, either. What would Dad and Mama think if I went topless!

There was only one way to make everything right again and to make up for the grief I had caused my parents: if I could show them that I really did deserve to live, then they would have to accept that I couldn't be with them now.

I crossed my fingers. I swore a solemn oath. Then I fell asleep, exhausted.

After that, I began showing up less frequently for our Wednesday night rendezvous at the hollow tree. At first I was still occasionally tempted — I'd have loved to watch Gerda's stubby fingers roll a joint for the three of us, or to collapse against Marlies in helpless laughter. But it did get easier, and soon enough neither of them wanted to be my friend anymore. With wounded faces they hissed I was a goody-goody, a traitor, because I never waited for them in the dark anymore, stamping my feet against the cold. The prospect of the three of us sitting together on a beach some day, waiting for photographers, soon became a most unlikely scenario. Yet I was never completely sure if I was doing the right thing. I often found myself glancing over my shoulder, my heart racing, thinking I could hear my parents' hurried footsteps.

My father was a dyed-in-the-wool hiker. He was the proud owner of a pair of walking boots sturdy enough to climb Mount Everest, and a pair of baggy knickers no normal person would ever be caught dead wearing. Every Sunday he'd be at it again. His favorite stomping ground was an expanse of dunes near our house, a rambling nature preserve. Dad knew its entire topography by name: the Tuna Can, Rosewater Field, Mustard Grove, the Orange Bowl, the Duckflats. He never kept to the trails marked with little colored arrows; that was for fair-weather dabblers only. For hours at a time he would tramp enthusiastically over hills and through dales full of hawthorn, wild roses, and rabbit holes, with the rest of us trailing in his wake, plaintively wondering how much farther it was. It made no difference if it rained, or if you got your ankle caught in a poacher's trap. You were expected to go along, no matter what. "Kester, my boy," my father said cheerfully, "you'd have found some other way to sprain that ankle of yours anyway. You children are always complaining about *something*."

One advantage of Ida's arrival, I decided, was that because of her stroller, at least we had to stick to the paths. I loathed having to trudge through deep sand drifts, and I was always afraid that my father's inner compass would some day fail him in the middle of nowhere.

In November my mother finally put an end to our Sunday tradition. "You keep warm because you keep moving, but Ida has to lie there for hours in her stroller, turning blue with cold," she announced after breakfast. She gave the cradle beside her chair a gentle nudge to start it rocking. Ida was making contented little noises, expectant grunts and gurgles.

"We'll just bundle her up well," said my father. He was already lacing up his hiking boots. We each had a pair, brown leather with red laces. You had to rub them with lashings of moldy-smelling grease, otherwise the leather developed sharp cracks that sliced right through your socks and into your flesh.

"I won't hear of it," said my mother. "And Michael is staying in today as well, with that nasty cough. If he's coming down with a cold, I don't want him giving it to Ida."

Carlos looked delighted. "Then I can go play with my trains."

"No, you are under quarantine, young man. You'll stay in bed until you are no longer contagious. And Kester will ride his bike over to the drugstore in a little while, to fetch some cough medicine for you. Frits, have a look in the paper, will you, and tell me which pharmacy is open . . ."

"But there's nothing wrong with that child. He can't possibly infect Ida," said my father, bristling. "Margje, I do wish you would stop —"

"I'm not going to go to bed, Mama, do you hear?" Carlos cried.

"I'll stay home and play with you," Billie offered sanctimoniously.

"Sybille," my father said brusquely, "put on your boots." He turned to my mother. He looked about to fly into a rage. "So what are your plans then?"

"I'll have to stay home with Ida."

"But if we just take her with us, the problem's solved."

My mother slammed down the breakfast dishes she had just stacked. "All you ever think of is yourself. Do you want her to come down with something?"

"If Kester doesn't have to go, then I'm not coming either," said Billie. "I die of embarrassment in these dorky boots."

My father snapped at my mother, "There is nothing wrong with Ida except that you're hovering over her all day like a broody hen. We're all going out for a walk, and that's that."

Ida began to cry, bleating like a little goat.

"You see?" My mother lifted the baby out of the crib and clutched her to her breast. Her voice turned shrill. "Just *go*, why don't you, for Christ's sake. Sybille, do as your father says and put on your shoes. You too, Ellen, get a move on."

I was so flustered I nearly couldn't get my laces tied. When she put on that new voice of hers, I just lost it. The creepiest thing was that she hardly moved her lips. Like a ventriloquist.

We filed out of the house shortly afterward, just the three of us, an unusually short and subdued procession. We had to battle the wind on the Zandvoorterweg, and by the time we reached the entrance to the dunes, my nose was beginning to run. My father turned left along the drainage canal, which was choppy with foam. Billie and I exchanged worried glances: that meant a forced march to Birdsong, or perhaps even as far as the Bracken.

A formation of cackling terns swooped over the water. My father walked a few yards ahead of us, his head tucked between his shoulders. We had to step up the pace to keep up with him. I fervently tried to imagine myself as a brave soldier at the battle of Thermopylae. According to Herodotus, our enemy, the Persians, had such flimsy heads that their skulls would shatter if you just tossed a pebble at them. That was because the Persians always wore those felt hats. In order to develop a rock-hard head, you had to expose it to the elements. Still, I wasn't about to take off my hood.

Near the Scallop Ford, Billie yanked at my sleeve, making me stop. "That jerk doesn't even know we're here," she hissed. "We might as well turn around and go home."

"We *can't!*" I answered in a whisper.

"Watch me," said Billie. In a flash she disappeared among the tall naked trunks of the pine forest. "Billie, come back!" I urged, as loudly as I dared. The trees creaked loudly in the wind. A flock of crows overhead uttered raw, hoarse shrieks.

My heart was banging in my throat. I was the cement: I had to keep everyone together. It simply wasn't right for me to be the only one left. My father would look around, and he would see nobody but me. His face would crumple with disappointment: only Ellen. Still, there was nothing to do but to start moving again. Stumbling, I followed his silent silhouette.

We trudged over a sandbank colonized by sparse clumps of beach grass. Next we crossed a field of gorse. A pheasant whirred out of the underbrush when it heard me: I was stomping my feet so hard that it sounded as if there were at least six of me.

At first I kept a respectful distance. But the likelihood kept growing that my father would say something intended for both Billie and me. "Look, this is where the central dunes start. You can tell from the deciduous trees." That would be a sign he was beginning to snap out of his grouchy mood. When he was in good spirits, he always liked to explain things.

Panting, I caught up with him. "Seen any deer yet?" I demanded urgently.

He didn't answer. But after a little while he took my hand and tucked it together with his own into the warm pocket of his overcoat. "What do you think, Ellen," he finally asked, staring straight ahead, "is

Mama right, is it true I only ever think of myself?"

Oh no, Dad, it's not true, you're the best. But that was something I would never dare say out loud. We'd both have died of embarrassment.

The wind swept up the clouds, clearing a trail of pale blue in the sky. In the distance, the sun was grimly trying to break through. A shaft of dim light slipped over the hill ahead of us. "Look at that moss," said my father, standing still. "Isn't it a shame Ida has to miss this. I took each one of you to this spot when you were little, even in winter. But perhaps you didn't appreciate it at all. Perhaps you'd rather have done something more . . . interesting." The last came out as a sneer. He let go of my hand.

Once at dinner, not long ago, he had hurled a pan of stewed endive at my head after I remarked that having your nose buried in old newspapers all day could make your brain go soft. It had been Kester, seated next to me, who had taken the full brunt of the steaming vegetables; the pan shattered his plate into smithereens, and Carlos, who'd burst out laughing, had been sent to bed with a good spanking.

My mother said later that I'd better never, ever, get it into my head again to belittle my father. As a young boy, he'd had to ride around in his father's vegetable cart, and in order to provide us with a better life than he'd had, he worked himself to the bone, six days a week. "The fact that you are learning Greek, young lady," she fumed, "doesn't give you the right to look down on your father. Don't you ever let me catch you at it again."

All I'd actually been trying to do was express concern over the fact that my father was always working. He probably looked forward all week to his Sunday outing with us, when he could finally gulp in some fresh air and shake all that dust from the U.S. of A. out of his head.

"We *are* going as far as Birdsong, aren't we, Dad?" I chirped.

"Well, what about you, Sybille?" said my father, turning around. "Are you up for . . . Hey, where *is* that little minx?"

"Billie!" I shouted for form's sake, as loudly as I could, but fear made my voice thin and shrill. Instead of blowing his top over my sister's getaway, all the color drained out of my father's face. "When did you last see her?"

I shuffled my feet guiltily. "At the Scallop Ford."

"Goddamn it, that's over half an hour

ago! Couldn't you have told me I was walking too fast?" He grabbed me by the shoulders. "Now she's lost us and is wandering around somewhere all by herself!"

I was sure she was already home, with a nice cup of cocoa and the latest teen fan magazine.

"I'll never forgive myself if something's happened to her."

I was burning with shame. "She knows the way back, Dad. From the Scallop Ford, it's only —"

"I can't have my daughters traipsing around in the wilds on their own. You are much too pretty."

That declaration threw me for a loop. Why, would my father prefer us to look different, then? It always gave me a thrill when the boys whistled at Billie in the street, and I couldn't wait for the time when I too would make them crash their bikes into a pole, just by flashing them a smile.

"Maybe we can get the park ranger to help," my father said tersely. "Come, Ellen, let's cut through here, it'll save time." He stuffed my ponytail into my hood and took my hand again. We crossed Twisted-Tree Field, Clogs Pan, Flea Corner, and Crow's Copse, and then crossed to the other side of the canal, over the stone bridge. Every step of the way felt as if my heart were being skewered on meat hooks. If I told on Billie, she'd be in big trouble. But how could I just let my father make himself sick with worry for no reason? He looked about ready to call in the helicopters and the bloodhounds.

"What's he thinking of, does he think we're in Oklahoma City or something?" Billie whispered into my middle ear, the spot where I'd once had an ear infection and which still felt as spongy as a Persian skull. "He's about to make a complete ass of himself, the sucker. Wait and see."

"Dad!" I managed, as my father stepped up to the park rangers' stone hut at the exit, next to the ticket machine.

He turned around, his hand poised by the bell: a long, skinny man in baggy knickers, a pair of binoculars dangling around his neck, windblown hair plastered over his pate.

"Dad, she just went home!"

"Let's hope so, but —"

"No, really! She turned back at the Scallop Ford because she . . . because she was cold."

He leaned forward and brought his face right up to mine. "She said that? That she was cold?"

"Yes!"

"Did she really say that, Ellen?"

I felt so bad I started to cry.

"She'd forgotten her hat, Dad!"

"And how come neither of you had the courage to tell me?" He straightened up. "Am I such a monster?" He raised his hand to his head in a dazed gesture. And at that moment, I knew with absolute certainty that in my entire life I would never find anyone capable of such forgiveness. In the end, Dad would always absolve me of absolutely anything. I really needed to tell him right then and there that he was the best father in the whole wide world, but the words would not come out.

Bending down again, he shook me gently. "Come on, Ellen, it isn't really worth all the tears, now is it? I bet Mama is waiting for us with fishcakes."

Sunday was fishcake day.

He cupped my face in his hands. "Loyalty, my love," he said, "is a virtue. But being loyal's not always easy. You have to learn to choose. And to be very careful when making that choice."

The human mind works in merciful ways: when there's trouble brewing, you're

187

never obliged to take in all at once what fate has up its sleeve, even if the signs are staring you in the face. Awareness is usually doled out to you in small, measured doses. The drawback, of course, is that things can go from bad to worse without your ever noticing it.

If my father was annoyed at my mother for never showing her face in the office again after Ida's arrival, he certainly managed to keep it under his hat. We didn't notice anything different about him, except that he pulled up his chair to his desk even earlier in the morning and got up from it even later at night. When I came to give him a kiss after school, I noticed that he was falling further and further behind with the files, now that he had the added job of keeping the card index current as well.

Esmée had been excused from some of her clipping duties so that she could assist clients on the telephone. Bas had been entrusted with keeping Esmée's clippings up to date in his spare time, but since he insisted on reading every article all the way through instead of confining himself to the headlines, the stacks of newspapers piled on his desk kept growing. This made him so nervous that he kept connecting people to the wrong extensions, was late with his tea and coffee rounds, and forgot to order new office supplies in time. "It's a madhouse in here," he'd complain, red in the face. "You're better off as a galley slave."

Marie-Louise, too, openly sulked as she pored over her beauty pageants and Emmy Awards. Her scissors needed replacing, the toilet paper had run out again, and there was never any yogurt in the refrigerator these days.

One of the other student interns left, giving neither notice nor a reason: that quiet boy who covered Science and Technology, and just as NASA was getting ready to send a space probe to Mars, too. There were unhappy rumblings from Culture and Sports as well.

My father gave in to Esmée's sighs and hired a temp.

"But we're still shorthanded," said Esmée ungratefully when Kester and I came to pick up her packages in the late afternoon. "So when's your mother coming back to work?"

That became a familiar refrain, one that we had to listen to over and over again. I sat on the stairs with Orson, racking my brains. If only someone could relieve my mother of her worry over Ida. If only someone could convince her that the baby was perfectly healthy, then she'd finally be able to concentrate on normal life again. But who was there who could do that? She no longer had any faith in our family doctor. He had long ago stopped rushing over at every frantic phone call. And to her outrage, the last time he had written out two prescriptions, not for Ida, but for *her!* Valium and sleeping pills. As if she needed them! The medicine bottles that Billie had picked up from the pharmacy remained untouched on the bathroom counter.

Orson rested his heavy head on my knee and gazed up at me hopefully. Because of Ida, I had to keep him on a leash, even indoors. He did his best to become invisible when he heard my mother's voice or her footsteps. He had taken her remarks about a dog kennel in the backyard to heart. He was crawling with germs, Mama said.

"You're in the way, child," said my father, coming up the stairs with a stack of files. I could see clippings messily sticking out of the bulging folders, as if the entire chaos of the U.S. of A. were scrambling into position to fight its way out as soon as my father relaxed his grip some more: serial killers, 42nd Street hookers, corrupt policemen, homeless winos and all. "You've got to hold on to those folders good and tight," I said anxiously.

He gave me a little pat on the top of my head and stepped over Orson. "Don't you have any homework to do? Then please go and see if your mother needs help with anything."

I took Orson down to Bas, who was sweating over a mountain of newspapers. "A senator having an affair with his secretary, would that be one of mine, or is that Marie-Louise's department?" he asked me, stricken.

The telephone rang. He pushed the buttons. "Bureau Van Bemmel. Yes, I'll connect you with Mrs. De Vries."

Were people no longer asking for my mother, then?

"Esmée," Bas mouthed into the receiver, "it's that joker from the *Volkskrant* again." He hung up. "He calls at least six times a day, that one. I think he wants her." With a sigh, he picked up his scissors again.

My mother was sitting in the sunroom with Ida on her lap. I hesitated in the doorway, to gauge her mood. She was stroking Ida's little head with slow, pensive motions. Then she saw me. "Look who's here," she cooed gaily at the baby.

"Hi, Mama," I said, relieved, and sat down on one of the creaky wicker chairs.

There was a pot of tea on a tea-warmer. It was only half past four, but it was already getting dark. My favorite time of day. I suddenly cheered up completely. It was too bad for my father and for the staff, of course, but what could be nicer than having a cup of tea with your own mother? I was convinced that this was how it was done in other families.

"Will you braid my hair?" I asked. "Look, starting up here."

"Oh, you mean the way Sybille wore hers last time? Come here then."

I squeezed in next to her. Ida squawked and went for my sleeve. She reeked of the salve Mama had been rubbing into her head, a nasty smell like chlorine or something you used to disinfect the toilet bowl. If my little sister ever found out that all her troubles in her short little life were my fault, she'd make me pay, and how. I pushed her chubby little hand away impatiently.

"Hey, Ellen, don't be so mean to her," said my mother.

"She's pulling at me."

"You were always so sweet to Michael, but you can't even manage a smile for Ida. How come?"

I shrugged.

She began braiding my hair. "You aren't jealous, are you?"

"Mama, please. This is so cozy, sitting here together like this, and then you start giving me an earful."

"I would so like you to love Ida as well."

"Can't we give her another name?" I asked.

"Would that help, do you think?"

Turning to her, I nodded fervently.

She raised her eyebrows, tickled. "And what should we call her, then?"

I looked at Ida. She stared back at me earnestly with her big dark eyes. And then suddenly, I saw who she really was, deep down inside. She was desperately waving her clenched fists. Save me, Ellen!

"Sophie," I whispered, elated. Sophie rhymed with Tweedledum and Tweedledee. Sophie was a perfect name for a sister. With a Sophie, you didn't need to worry. Sophies had no mischief in them.

The baby crowed, sputtering.

"Well, I think she likes it," said my mother.

I was so excited that I bit the inside of my cheek. "It isn't too late, Mama. She hasn't been properly christened yet, since that time you —"

My mother stiffened suddenly. "God, I

completely forgot! Of course — she still needs to be christened! Suppose something should happen to her, frail little thing that she is, and she hasn't even been baptized! She'll go straight to hell!"

I stared at her uncertainly. It wasn't like my mother to be worrying about hell.

She pushed me off. "Go fetch Daddy, quick. We must take care of this right now."

My father would say she was totally nuts. There would be such a row that all the windows would rattle. I could have kicked myself for getting her into one of her terrible states again. With all the conviction I could muster, I breathed, "We could do it ourselves. It's true, Mama, you're allowed to, in an emergency, I learned about it at school. In an emergency you're allowed to do it yourself, on board ship and that sort of thing, or if —"

"So!" she interrupted me sharply. "Finally I'm not the only one! You see it too, now — that Ida is an emergency case." Her eyes glittered feverishly.

I felt the braid slipping out of my hair. Haltingly I said, "Her name is Sophie."

My mother waved me aside. Dipping her fingers in her half-empty teacup, she sprinkled my sister's forehead with the tea. "I

194

christen you in God's name, I . . . What else should I say?"

"That's fine," I stammered.

"Are you sure?"

I hesitated. She hadn't yet said: I christen you Sophie.

My mother demanded urgently, "So does she now have her own guardian angel?"

"Yes," I said gratefully. My father needn't ever find out about this. "Yes, Mama, don't worry, nothing bad can happen to her now."

They say pregnant women drift around blissfully on cloud nine, patting their whale-bellies, yet all I seem able to do is picture my delicate little Ida-Sophie dying, dying over and over again — asphyxiating from a lack of oxygen, starving for want of nourishment. She's an inert stone in the pit of my stomach, lifeless, a petrified child, a fossil. Sometimes my fears get the better of me. Is she not destined for this world, then? Is that it? Is it she who has been banging on my placenta with her little shrimp fists in an effort to expel it, so that she may return to the peaceful twilight place whence she came? Is Ida-Sophie al-ready fed up with life? Is she a wish that will never come true, a story that lacks an ending; is she meant to live amid the stars, and not among humankind?

The walls come pressing in on me. The ceiling sags a yard and a half lower. My mattress is a bed of nails. Oh, little girl, just give me one chance, just let me give you life! We'll buy red, blue, and yellow poster paints and big pieces of paper. I'll give you twenty-five cents for every jar of acorns you collect in the garden; we'll get a dog; I already know what we'll call him — there's so much to do together.

"Your mail," says Lucia, entering my room without knocking. Her eldest, Samantha, dark ratty hair cut short, clings to her thigh. A high-strung child who can't bear to let her mother out of her sight. Lucia raps her sharply on the fingers; Samantha lets go. She looks at me distraught.

"Come over here," I say. I pick up the bottle of perfume that stands on my night table. "See how nice this smells."

The little girl allows me to spray a little puff on her wrist and sniffs at it. One corner of her mouth curls up. She's practically smiling.

"Don't you want your mail?" Lucia demands, pushing the girl away, out of my reach.

I hold out my hand for the postcard she's waving at me. She holds it up a little higher. Articulating elaborately, she reads: *"Dear Ellen, I must speak to you urgently."*

I grab the card out of her hand. It's signed *Wrm grtngs,* just like that other one, long ago. I become furious. "No one would write that just for a lark! He could be in trouble. Do you really expect me to turn my back on my friends — for you?"

"It's against the agreement." I can detect something close to triumph glittering in her eyes: no longer at the mercy of someone else's moods, she is now the one pulling the strings.

"He doesn't have to come here," I say, as reasonably as I can. "I can just phone him."

"Ellen van Bemmel speaking," she says, cradling an imaginary receiver to her ear. It's uncanny, the way she manages to make her voice sound like mine.

I am beset by claustrophobic despair. More than two weeks to go before Jan Bramaan will permit me even to sit up with my legs dangling over the edge of the bed. Sixteen times twenty-four more hours flat on my back, and that on top of the twenty-eight days I've already spent that way; a mountain of enforced bed rest still looms ahead of me. At least another two months to go before Bramaan will let me get out and take care of myself again, if everything goes well, that is. "I can't just keep giving the guy the brush-off! I'm telling you, if he doesn't hear from me, he'll be standing on our front steps one of these days. Is *that* what you want?"

"Don't think I would open the door if someone rang the bell," says Lucia.

"Who's coming?" Samantha asks. She is sitting on the foot of the bed and now opens the photo album Ida-Sophie and I were leafing through earlier.

"The goddamn plumber!" I yell, losing my self-control. "It's been weeks now, dammit, that I've been lying here in this rotten stench because your mother refuses to have anything done about that blocked drain. And this is *my* house, I'll have you know."

"You're kidding," says Lucia.

"Look, Mama, it's the same house," says Samantha, turning a page.

Lucia glances at the photos. Her otherwise inscrutable face turns openly hostile. So Ellen van Bemmel had a happy childhood on top of it all, complete with family snapshots. It's the last straw.

Seeing that friendship isn't in the cards

for us anyway, I resume, "Listen, to get back to that friend of mine —"

"Have you considered that we are just as cut off here from everything and everyone as you are? I can't just pick up the phone and have a chat with one of my girlfriends either. Anyway, if you were away on vacation, you couldn't be expected to respond to his card, now could you?"

"But he knows I'm here! He's already had me on the phone once!"

"He dialed a wrong number."

"Come on, do you seriously believe he won't have recognized my voice? For Christ's sake! Can't I just tell him I can't see him right now? Really, I think you're overreacting."

She puts her hands on her hips. "I'm not staying in this house a minute longer if I can't be one hundred percent sure that it's safe. And don't forget that you can't even wipe your own butt right now." She yanks her daughter off the bed by one arm.

"I want to look at the pictures!" cries Samantha.

In a spirit of conciliation, I offer, "Why don't you leave her here?" Having to lie here sixteen times twenty-four hours, with only my own thoughts to keep me company, no distractions other than those frigging Kegel exercises Jan Bramaan is having me do — suddenly it's more than I can bear. A little girl's company would be a relief.

Taking her time, Lucia looks me up and down. Finally she says, "The children are not allowed in your room. You need your rest." She purses her lips contemptuously.

"Lucia," I plead. "Can't we —"

"A truce?" asks Billie. "Is that what you're proposing?" She is sitting on the windowsill, one leg slung over the other, in her Indian cotton dress. Her shapely legs are tanned. She's wearing sandals, as if she's just come from the beach.

"Poor Ellen," says Kes, looming up beside my sister. "You're bored out of your skull, aren't you? Don't forget, you've always got Billie and me."

"Can't we what?" Lucia inquires.

Kester's eyes twinkle at me. He zips his lips shut with his forefinger, the way we used to do: *My lips are sealed.*

"Nothing," I tell Lucia. "I'll call if I need you." I wave at her daughter. "Bye, Sam. See you later."

"Her name is Samantha," snaps Lucia.

When they are gone, I grab my album. That smile of Kester's. It's in one of the pictures. Yes, here it is! I knew it.

Thanksgiving at our house. Bureau van Bemmel's annual dinner in honor of the U.S. of A. We always had turkey and potato purée (*maaashed potaaatoes,* we'd drawl); my father would make a speech at least six words long; my mother would pour the cider and Marie-Louise would get a little tipsy and do her Marilyn Monroe impression.

Bas is seated next to me, wearing a Stars and Stripes shirt bigger than the entire North American continent. He is twenty-four; I am twelve. I'm ignoring him. In the picture it's clear all my attention is focused on my mother. Please, Mama, don't start acting weird again tonight.

By that time, she must have christened my sister at least five, six times. Possibly even more, when I wasn't around. I was terrified someone would find out. If only I hadn't put the idea into her head! And she had her nose constantly buried in our black linen Bible, which in the past had gathered mildew quietly on the shelf. Afterward she'd say she had a headache, and Dad would tell us to be quiet.

I wouldn't have minded, actually, if Dad had come to find out about it, about the christenings and everything — but not if it meant getting in trouble for it.

While I was keeping an anxious eye on my mother at our Thanksgiving party, Bas was taking advantage of the opportunity to nab a piece of turkey off my plate. The camera caught him at it red-handed. My brother saw it too: he smirked and said nothing. Bas is grinning at the prospect of seeing me find my plate empty and looking around me perplexed.

"Bas!" I mutter, my cheek pressed into the pillow, my arm stretched out. I remain that way for some time. Then I turn over onto my back with a sigh.

Kick me, Ida-Sophie; show me you're still in there and that you're longing to be born.

What did you say? You want to see the picture with the apples?

My daughter isn't even born yet, but she's already bursting with questions. "Don't I have a grandma then, Mama? What about a grandpa? Don't I have a family? Why not?"

I give in, for the umpteenth time. Obediently I turn the heavy pages of the photo album, in search of the picture of my mother with the apples.

She is carefully putting the apples Sybille just bought into the fruit bowl, one by one.

Golden Delicious, pale and waxy to the touch. They fill her with disgust. They don't smell nice, either. "What kind of garbage did you let them sell you *this* time?" she asks her daughter, who is unpacking the rest of the groceries.

"They were on the list," Sybille answers indignantly.

Click goes the camera.

"Come on, Ellen, you're getting in our way with that thing."

"Dad said I could finish the film," says Ellen.

"Then do it somewhere else."

Sybille turns around, holding a leek. "Take one of me, Ellen. Go ahead." With a pious flourish she raises the leek heavenward, tilting her head sideways and closing her eyes. "I will watch over you, Sophie! Day or night, I will be your guardian angel!"

Margje has to repress a sudden urge to slam her two daughters' grinning heads together. How dare they — the nerve of those brats! She yanks the leek out of Sybille's hands. It walks around dressed like a slut, in a skirt that's obscenely short and that V-neck slashed down to her navel, and then dares to make fun of the holy sacraments! Suddenly she notices a mark on her daughter's neck. "What's that? Have you been letting some boy suck on you again?"

Sybille's hand goes to her throat. She blushes. Uncertainly, she begins to giggle.

"You're grounded for the rest of the week. And go put on some decent clothes."

"But, Mama —"

"You heard me. Out of my sight. And that goes for you too, Ellen. Yes, *you*. I never have a moment's peace in my own house."

She is still shaking when her daughters have slammed the kitchen door behind them with a crash. For months she's been stumbling about in the dark, but now she can see. How can she have been so blind? Sybille's apples: a sign from God, surely, who had to banish Eve from His paradise.

She picks up the fruit bowl. It's so heavy it gives her a start. It feels as if she's holding the sins of all mankind in her hands. She must be right, then.

Outside, by the garbage can, she has a better idea. She takes a shovel from the shed, goes to the farthest corner of the garden, digs a deep hole, and hastily buries the apples in it. Now she must take care that Ida's cradle never lines up with this particular spot.

She runs up to the bathroom and fills the baby bath. Ida squawks a little at being roused from her sleep at this unusual hour. Her mouth begins to pucker but then lets out an acquiescent sigh. Margje quickly peels off her pink stretchie. From now on Ida will wear only white, and she'll sleep under a white quilt. All the other bedding will be buried exactly eight yards from the apples, one for every cardinal sin, plus another one for good measure.

She walks to the bathroom with the naked infant in her arms. She checks the water temperature. It's a little on the warm side, but surely hell is much hotter. It's all so clear to her now. As clear as glass. The knowledge gives her a wonderful sense of peace.

Calmly she lowers Ida into the water. "Don't cry," she says softly as the child begins screeching. Her skin promptly turns bright red. "I baptize you in God's name," says Margje as she pushes the baby's little head under. "I absolve your soul of all sin." For a moment she sees Ida's entire happy future life pass before her eyes, as if in a movie. Pure as a little angel, inviolate, she is. The apple of God's eye. But wait . . . apple? Eye? Alarmed, she pulls the child out of the water. It's howling, it's squeezing tears out of eyes that are pinched shut. So *that's* where the sin lies hidden, the sin that will be her undoing!

Instinctively she pats her clothing. Doesn't she have a safety pin somewhere that she can use to poke out those dark pupils?

Loud music blares from the attic. Her children are roaring along, wild and rebellious. Sybille's clear voice, Ellen who can never carry a tune: *"I once met the devil; he was mighty sick."*

She slaps her hands over Ida's ears. She presses as hard as she can on both sides of the little head.

"Why is she crying so?" It's her husband's voice, suddenly coming up behind her. Concerned or irritated, she's not quite sure which. She has to concentrate hard in order to deal with his sudden presence. It's as if she has to gather herself from the four corners of her body and piece herself together again bit by bit. Here — left leg, liver, fingernails . . . OK, OK, and now, last but not least, my heart.

"The water may be just a little on the warm side," she says.

"But it's nowhere near time for her bath!" He looks at her in surprise.

"She had such a dirty diaper." She lifts

the baby out of the water and wraps her in a towel. Water gushes out of Ida's mouth. She hiccups a few times and utters a few more pathetic wails.

"Here, give her to me." He takes the child from her. He is an expert father. He never forgets the talcum powder for the little bottom and knows how to fold a diaper with one hand.

Together they have raised an entire family. She'd like to lean against him for a bit, put her head on his shoulder. He is her rock. Her husband, her friend, the father of her children.

Her lover!

All the blood rushes to her head. Could it be that it is they who are the culprits, the depraved source of all wickedness?

"I'm so frightened," she mumbles.

"Darling." The irritation in his voice is now unmistakable. "Really, you're worrying yourself sick over nothing. You have a child that's healthy as an ox. Wiersma says the same thing, and that man sees hundreds of infants every year. I wish you would —"

"I'm not making it up," she says sharply.

He pins the diaper in place. He has narrow hands; his nails are always cut very short. These are the hands she has permitted to touch her flesh all these years — she didn't know any better. Involuntarily she takes a step backward.

Right then and there it's final. It's neither a question nor a consideration; it's a decision: no more sex. Ever. For Ida's sake.

"What do you want her to wear?" he asks.

She grabs a white sweater. "I'll do it."

"Margje," he says, reluctantly handing Ida back to her, "I'm only asking you to put all this nonsense out of your head. It's so unlike you. Pull yourself together. You do have four other children, you know, and there's piles of work waiting for you in the office."

He sees but he is blind; he hears but he is deaf. He is no longer her ally.

In the attic they're playing the same blasphemous Blood, Sweat & Tears record again. Again her children sing at the top of their voices that they have met the devil. *Mighty sick was he.* Sickness, then, must be a sign of his presence! There is the proof: Ida has indeed been possessed by the devil. He has given himself away. Now she knows what she has to do. She will drive him out single-handedly to make her daughter strong and healthy again.

What was going through my father's

mind? He must have been hurt by my mother's sudden inexplicable coolness, the way she pushed him away when he tried to caress her during the day, the abrupt way she turned her back on him in bed at night.

Frits van Bemmel, man of the world?

Ha! Haha!

But every marriage has its low points, surely; there is more to marriage, by definition, than the mere coupling of two bodies. Perhaps he could consult their family doctor, but he doesn't really like to bother him. Besides, when he considers how to phrase his question, the words stick in his throat. He wouldn't want to give the doctor the impression he's some kind of randy old goat. *All you ever think of is yourself.*

So he just sits and waits, week after excruciating week. The daylight hours find him seated at his desk, labeling the contents of his folders in his neat script, always able to come up with just the right word to describe every human deed or misdeed. And at night he casts down his eyes as Margje sits at the dressing table in her nightgown, brushing her hair. Once, the very sight of her was enough to bring all the holy statues in the church to a state of arousal. How can he be expected to remain unmoved in her presence, he who is not made of stone?

His own body seems strange to him, now that it is no longer defined by its intimacy with hers. Was his chest always this puny, his knees always so knobby? In the privacy of the bathroom he clumsily massages his swollen member. His scrotum is heavy, distended. Embarrassed, he urinates hurriedly.

For over sixteen years she has been reading his mind, so surely tomorrow, or at the very least the day after, she will notice how much he wants her, and she'll go back to being the warm Margje he used to know.

He lies in bed, drained. She cleans off her face with lotion, then rubs in a night cream, and he pretends to be asleep. She gets up, her breasts clearly visible under the thin cotton of her nightgown. She leans over the crib at the foot of the bed and whispers something into Ida's ear.

Perhaps the tide will turn once the baby moves up to the attic with the other children.

"Are you asleep?" she asks softly.

"Not anymore," he replies, briefly brimming with foolish hope.

"Never mind. I just thought you were asleep, that's all."

He thinks: Because if I were asleep you could get into bed beside me without having to worry. Now you'll be obliged to walk around jiggling Ida up and down in your arms for fifteen minutes or so, in the hope that I won't be able to keep my eyes open that long. Suddenly his heart goes out to her. "I'm sure I'll be out for the count as soon as I close my eyes," he promises, his throat constricting with tenderness.

"I'm just going downstairs with Ida for a bit. I think she's thirsty."

"Don't wear yourself out, Margje."

She is already out the door.

He turns over onto his back and shuts his eyes. A troubling thought: She was never this cold before Ida's arrival. She never behaved like this after any of the others. If she had acted this way after every pregnancy, it would have been a different matter, but it's only since Ida — Ida who is sucking Margje dry, so all that's left for him is ashes and ice. If Ida had never been born . . . He quickly tries to shake off the thought. Without Ida they would now be normally . . . He sits up and switches on the light. If Ida hadn't happened: How could you have such thoughts about your own flesh and blood? And then, an even more insane thought flashes through his head: Is the child really his?

No. No! He's just a little overtired, that's all.

He stretches out again, his hands behind his head. He makes an effort to bring his little daughter's features to mind, but instead he sees Sybille as a baby, her eyes burning with curiosity, the perfect oval of her little skull. The shape of her head. God in heaven, that's it. That's what Margje has been getting herself so worked up over. It's the shape of Ida's little head that gives her away.

All this time, then, her fussing and worrying has been nothing but a pretext, a tactic to prevent him from discovering that the child doesn't look anything like him. From early morning until late at night she has been keeping Ida hidden in her arms, and justifying it with her ridiculous fabrications about the baby's health.

Her own husband leaves her cold now, and the business they struggled so hard to build up together doesn't interest her anymore either: only a gullible dupe like Frits van Bemmel could miss the signs staring him right in the face.

Cuckold. Ludicrous wimp.

Who knows what she's up to every day, during the long hours when the office is busy and the children are at school? Her eyes, bloodshot with lust, leering as she bends over the other man. Her moist thighs spread wide. Her nipples hard with desire. The whole of her familiar, willing, eager body: scorn rises from every pore. That Frits, poor old fool. Confidently, she murmurs with glistening lips, "He'll never find out, not in a million years."

He flings the covers aside.

He's on his feet next to the bed, in a daze. I am your husband. You belong to me. He lurches toward the weedy figure with the puny chest looming up in the dressing-table mirror and punches him in the mouth. Glass splinters onto the floor. His knuckles are bleeding. These hands, Margje, are the ones that have always lifted you up on a pedestal. Don't ever forget that. I'm warning you. I'm warning you just this once.

In a little while she'll walk into our bedroom with her wretched little bastard. Then what? *You, you.* All right then, I'll forgive you. Only if you. Only if you never again. Leave our life the way it was.

Who's the man?

Do I know him?

A journalist?

A correspondent? "You're sensational, Beddy."

The door creaks open. His blood grows cold.

"Daddy?" whispers Ellen. Her face is white and drawn.

He feels naked, with only his pajama bottoms on. "How come you're not asleep?" he manages, covering his wounded hand with the good one. As long as she doesn't notice the broken mirror.

Timidly she steps into the bedroom. "Where is Mama?"

"You'd better get back to bed."

"I have to talk to Mama." She sits down on the foot of the bed and begins picking at her toes. Skinny, splayed toes. He glances down at his own feet.

"What's the matter?" He sits down next to her.

Bashfully she places a hand on her chest. "I think I'm getting . . ." Her voice trembles.

"Is something hurting you? Are you coming down with something?"

She shakes her head. Looks at him helplessly.

"OK, no guessing games, Ellen, in the

middle of the night."

"Feel it, then!"

"Where?"

She points.

He puts out a hand, then quickly pulls it back in alarm, before he's actually touched her. Now he's the one whose eyes are blinking desperately. When was the last time he saw her chaste child's body naked? "Oh, *that!*" he says stupidly. "Nothing to worry about."

"But Dad, I don't want to . . ." She begins to weep soundlessly.

His own helplessness makes him furious. "That's normal at your age! Come on, don't be so silly! I thought you were supposed to be the smartest one in your class?"

She hunches her shoulders to hide the minute swellings on her ribcage.

The alarm clock ticks away; it's seven after midnight. He is perched on the edge of his bed with his unhappy daughter. She has his toes, and with any luck she'll have her mother's figure. "Off to bed now, Ellen. And I don't want to see you whining about every little thing all the time; really, you *are* a crybaby."

She jumps up, skinny and pitiful. "I don't want to have breasts," she screams.

"You don't have to have any either, do you?"

Now that the word is out in the open, he grabs her by the arm. "Tomorrow you'll be quite happy about it, you'll see . . ."

She throws him a look of withering scorn. Then she runs out of the room.

It's half past one and Margje still hasn't come to bed. He has cleaned up the broken glass; he's dabbed iodine on his hand; he's put on a pajama top. He is sitting up in bed, his eyes fixed on the alarm clock. He is numb one minute, in a rage the next. It's a fury without shape or content, a pure seething, a storm, a tornado, a hurricane. In his calmer moments, a half-hearted epithet occasionally works its way out. *Slut.* He says it out loud, but it resists, it slips out of his grasp, it won't let itself be attached to Margje. It simply will not, obstinately, allow itself to be true. "Slut." Feebly he utters the word again. Name it first. Only that which is labeled can later be retrieved.

In his mind he tries to run through the entire archive of his marriage, but he keeps getting stuck, pointlessly, at her soup. Her everlasting soup. She fervently believes in its miraculous properties, for persons who are in the throes of a growth spurt, for persons in need of comfort, for young and for old: homemade meatballs, a handful of rice, fresh parsley from the garden, and a dollop of sour cream. When she's alone, she likes to eat it in bed, with the radio softly playing. She once told him that the soup turns out best when you make it with peace in your heart and a husband who doesn't resent having to scrub the pan afterward.

Jealousy makes his heart shrivel. Treachery. Breach of faith. Humiliation. Shame.

At two-fifteen she enters the bedroom. The baby is whimpering softly in her arms, almost breathless, as if she's been crying for hours. She comes to a halt in the middle of the room. She looks worn out; vertical grooves run down along the sides of her mouth.

"But Frits," she says, taken aback, "how come you're still up?" She eases the baby into the crib.

You thought you'd never get found out, but you were wrong; you underestimated me.

"My mirror!" She brings a hand to her mouth.

I'll show you what humiliation really means.

"Frits! How did my mirror get broken? What in heaven's name is going on?" She stands motionless, defenseless, her arms hanging by her sides.

The next instant she is on her back on the floor next to the dressing table and he is straddling her, his bare hands ripping her nightgown apart at the neckline. She has no time to react, he is already inside her and begins to thrust, deep and hard, the treatment she deserves, like an animal, like an animal he comes inside her, and then, the immediate, awful awareness that something irreparable has taken place. Limply he collapses on top of her with his full weight, crushing her in his arms.

She doesn't say a word.

He thinks, it just took a moment, what's one moment in an entire lifetime? Clumsily he starts stroking her back.

She pushes him off her, using all her strength. Silently she gets to her feet, wraps the torn nightgown around herself, and, quiet and composed, leaves the bedroom without a backward glance.

Appalled, he remains prone on the floor. He simply cannot move. His self-loathing keeps him pinned to the ground.

It feels as if no more than ten minutes have passed when the alarm clock rings.

He isn't even aware of having fallen asleep; besides, it seems highly unlikely that a new day can be starting, or that the sun can be in any mood to rise.

He will have to face her.

Stiffly he gets up to turn off the alarm. As soon as the noise stops, Ida begins to cry. He picks her up out of habit and starts to unpin her wet diaper. And then, another shock. The baby's lower belly is covered with large, purple bruises. As he stares at them stupidly, she kicks him with a tiny foot ending in splayed little toes. His eyes swivel from her belly to her foot and back again.

"Ida," he says. "My God, *Ida!*"

Has Margje been keeping this to herself because he is always pooh-poohing her anxiety? He groans as he returns the infant to the crib. The house is still quiet as a morgue. He dashes down the stairs three steps at a time, grabs the hall phone, and dials the doctor's number. Spontaneous hemorrhaging: it can only mean one thing.

"Van Bemmel speaking," he screams into the mouthpiece as soon as someone picks up on the other end. "Doctor, has our daughter Ida ever been checked for leukemia?"

# Ida
## (through Kester's telephoto lens!), winter 1972–1973

I can hear Lucia laughing downstairs in the kitchen with her children. It's a new and unfamiliar sound; I have to listen to it for a while with my eyes shut before I can place it. I try to picture the four of them having their breakfast around my battered pine table, breaking up with laughter. Has little Rochelle, still only a toddler, come out with something outrageously cute? Or was it Samantha . . .

I am dumbfounded. A guffawing Lucia. It comes close to turning my entire world order upside down. My next thought is even more upsetting: How long has it been since laughter was heard in this house? When was the last time that chairs were tilted up with glee? In all the months I've been living here, have the walls ever throbbed with the sounds of mirth, causing the plaster to flake off the ceiling?

Now I hear doors opening and slamming. Patches of sun suddenly dancing into rooms and corridors, making them come alive with light. The pounding of children's feet on the stairs. "No, *me* first!" It's as if I can suddenly feel it again myself, the friction of the banisters whizzing by under my backside. A crash, then another one.

"Careful!" calls Lucia. "Or it will end in tears."

A little later she comes into my room. I pretend to be asleep. When she puts the cup of coffee down next to me, I spy through my lashes that her face suddenly seems less puffy than before. What I had put down to bloating must have been bruises, then. She'd look quite nice if she had something done about her teeth.

She opens the venetian blinds, glances at the neglected garden, and clicks her tongue. Dear God, the repressed little housewife inside her must be stirring. Now that she has jarred the house awake, she's itching to get her hands on my garden as well, to plunge her spade left and right into the flower beds that never did get planted and are all overrun with weeds again. Lucia the good fairy. Don't make me laugh. What can she be thinking? She knows she can't even set foot in the yard;

she has surrendered her liberty of her own free will.

"Good morning," I say coldly.

"I made a pot of coffee. There was no tea left. Do you want to wash yourself now, or later?"

I nod at the chair by the window. One hour a day, Jan Bramaan granted me last week. We're making progress.

Lucia puts down the coffee cup on the windowsill, then helps me out of bed and assists me in navigating the crossing. We are getting better at this, I have to admit. Her hand firmly under my elbow, mine draped over her shoulder. My other hand holding my stomach. Stay put, Ida-Sophie. My legs are still mushy, and my head is spinning. Only when I've been sitting down for several minutes do I start feeling a little better.

While I sip my coffee, Lucia changes the bed. Suddenly she remarks, almost timidly, "The children really are beginning to return to normal."

"That's nice," I comment, for lack of something more enthusiastic to say.

"They've been through such a lot." She abandons the bed, comes over to the window, and leans against the windowsill, arms crossed. I quickly avert my eyes from the small, livid scars notching her skin, dozens of them: but it's too late, she has seen me staring and quickly rolls down her sleeves. Just like Carlos.

A thunderstorm promptly starts brewing at the back of my head: pulsing atoms dangerously compressing. Hastily I correct myself: no, not just like Carlos. Of course not. Lucia is different from us. Nobody has lived through what we lived through. We are the only ones who can understand each other.

God, I hope I'm not getting a migraine.

"I just wanted to say . . ." An embarrassed blush seeps along Lucia's jaw, making her look young and vulnerable. She coughs into her fist. ". . . that we're lucky to be here."

"You certainly have to work hard enough for the privilege," I say curtly.

She casts her eyes down. Then looks up again. "You really are a cold customer, aren't you?" she says, almost pityingly.

Her words cut me to the quick. It's not true.

"So here we are; we're stuck with each other, you and I," she resumes, "so why don't we try to make the best of it?"

"If you'll forgive me, isn't it just a little late in the game to start making nice?"

She laughs a little sheepishly. "Jesus, Ellen, I'm not exactly going through the easiest time of my life right now. It can make a person a little touchy, you know."

I'm not in the mood to kiss and make up. Next we'll start comparing notes on all the misery we've suffered. Gerda and Marlies used to enjoy that. "Now you tell us yours." I can still see their greedy faces.

Stubbornly she continues, "After all, we're in the same boat. Neither of us can get out of here." She cocks her head, almost imploringly.

"No kidding. But what's been bugging me for weeks is how come it's you and your kids that are the ones who are locked away like criminals? Shouldn't it be the other way around?"

She looks at me nonplussed.

"I mean, why do you put up with it?"

"Mama," Vanessa calls out, storming into the room, "in a while, can we —" She stops short, suddenly realizing that she is not supposed to be here. My private enclave. The last measly square footage in my own house that's still mine. Her little mouth forms a startled O. She is losing her baby teeth. The gap in her top teeth is an exact replica of Lucia's, only on a smaller scale — as if she's showing me that her filial allegiance knows no bounds.

"I'm coming," Lucia tells her. She turns back to me. "Of course it ought to be the other way around; it shouldn't be us hiding out here like this, but do you know what they tell you at the police station, when you say you want to press charges? 'Now, now, Ma'am, a complaint like this is a very serious matter. It's your children's father you're talking about here. What will they say if he lands in jail thanks to you?' And if you do take their advice and go home, scared to death, then the next time they'll say, 'Come come, it can't be all that bad, can it now? Didn't you end up going back to him, last time?' "

"You could get a divorce and start a new life somewhere else," I suggest. This is exactly the sort of conversation I had wanted to avoid, but I must confess I do get a cruel kick out of ramming Lucia's shortcomings down her throat. Hopefully that'll put the kibosh on her desire for a reconciliation. We'll never be friends, Lucia. There are worlds of differences between us.

"Easy for you to say," she says nastily.

"Oh, and how would you know that?"

"Well? Who's the one who's so hell-bent on having a baby on her own? As if that's such a brilliant idea! It's pretty selfish and irresponsible, if you ask me." She stomps back to the bed and begins tugging savagely at the sheets.

"Better no father at all than an abusive one."

Behind me, silence. She is casting about for new ammunition. I hear her pounding my pillow ferociously. Finally she says, "And after this one, you'll probably adopt another ten, right? Just like Mia Farrow. To show the world what a wonderful —"

I say coolly, "I don't really believe in adoption. I . . ." Carlos's image flashes before me, the time I brought him a little stuffed dog at his new parents' house. It wasn't a successful visit. Suddenly my eyes sting with tears.

"Oh no? What are you going to fill this great big barn of a place with, then? Or were you planning to rent out rooms to airline attendants?" Her voice is shrill, envious.

I don't even bother answering her. My plans for the house were set the moment I first walked back in here with the real estate agent. Enough space — finally! — for each of us to have our own room. The first floor is where Billie's boudoir will be, with grubby cotton balls strewn about the floor and movie-star posters on the walls. Next door, Kester's quarters, crammed with pipe wrenches and pliers and rusty screws and bolts sorted into old jars. For Ida-Sophie, that sunny room with the balcony on the south side, and for Carlos we'll keep the guest room always on standby. I'll stay here in Bas's cubicle, and the au pair we'll need when I go back to work can have the attic.

My Ida-Sophie will learn to roll marbles and play hopscotch on the checkered tiles of the entrance hall. When it rains and she can't play outside, we'll set up an obstacle course next to the stairway. Kes used to be a whiz at inventing challenges which only he would attempt. He dared himself to hang from his feet headfirst in the stairwell and walk down the handrail on his hands. *"When the going gets tough,"* he'd pant in English, all red in the face, *"the tough get going."*

"Look, Ellen," my brother said, "I've made her a fan."

We were both wearing nothing but T-shirts and underpants. The thermostat was set to a sweltering seventy-seven degrees. March was doing its thing outside: wet snow, rain, an occasional hailstorm. My mother said the heat was important for Sophie's health;

she wanted to see her "sweat it out."

Whenever I was about to pass out, I'd go and spend a few minutes in the office, where individual radiator thermostats were set to a more moderate level. "How sweaty you are, Ellen," Esmée would remark innocently. "Don't you ever stop running around?" I didn't dare tell her why I was so hot. I hoped she would stumble on the truth by herself: that she or one of the others would put two and two together, smell a rat, and realize that things were happening in our part of the house that scared me. That's what adults were for, the way I understood it.

But Esmée had stopped asking after my mother altogether. She was now accustomed to the fact that Mama never stuck her nose in there anymore.

"Pay attention, Ellen! Look, this part turns," said Kester, showing me the workings of the blades that were meant to provide our little sister with a little cool air. He looked at me expectantly.

It gave me the willies. Billie and I had put an ice pack on Sophie's chest once, but we had been caught red-handed. We'd been made to go and sit in the cellar until Mama decided we were her children again. Billie had had a pink lipstick on her; she used it to write *Kilroy was here* on the porous cellar walls. She acted as if it didn't bother her. But she had been saying things like "I *am* an idiot" a lot lately, and then her eyes would fill with tears, and you hardly ever saw the dimple in her cheek these days.

Carlos, who had come down seeking refuge from Sophie's crying, had accidentally delivered us from our purgatory.

"I don't think Mama will approve of your fan idea," I had to tell Kester regretfully. "The whole point is to make Sophie hot. It's supposed to make her get better."

My brother stared stonily at his ingenious contraption. Then he dashed the thing to the ground and stamped it to pieces.

"But we could have used it ourselves," I protested.

Kes snorted indignantly, and I felt like a heel for thinking only of myself. Dejectedly, I fetched Orson from his doghouse in the yard and I biked with him to the beach in the rain. I let him run practically as far as IJmuiden, but even then he hadn't had enough. I had a devil of a time getting him back on his leash.

It was only on the way back — night was falling fast — that his gallop slowed to a sluggish trot, which in turn degenerated into a reluctant sort of shuffle. Finally, at the corner of the Lijsterlaan, he demonstratively flopped down into a puddle. I had to get off my bike to haul him back onto his feet.

At the dark entrance to his doghouse, Orson dug in his heels. He howled and he growled and he even bared his teeth briefly. I quickly tossed a handful of dog biscuits inside. By the time my dog realized he'd been had, I had already clicked the gate shut behind him.

"Just think of the Spartans," I told him in a quavering voice. "Do you really think they could have won hegemony over the entire Peloponnese by sitting on down cushions by the fire?"

I dragged his bucket out of the shed, filled his bowl, and pushed it under the fence. For a doghouse, it wasn't bad at all. I had a black fingernail to show for it where I'd hit my thumb with the hammer when Kes and I built it. I really didn't need to feel guilty.

I realized I was shivering and burning up at the same time. If I was coming down with some sort of bug, there'd be hell to pay. But instead of going inside and putting on dry clothes, I stayed out there in the rain, next to Orson's house, staring back at our house.

It was almost dinnertime. On the first and second floors almost all the lights were out. The only room that still had a light on was my father's office. I could make him out sitting at his desk laden with folders as clearly as if I'd been squinting through Kester's new telephoto lens. He was using one hand to prop up his head, and the other one to write with. Then he looked up pensively and stared outside for a moment.

"Dad," I breathed, raising my hand involuntarily, but of course he couldn't see me, in the dark back yard. He turned back to his work. TRAIN WRECK IN MINNEAPOLIS. WOMEN'S LIB SELLS — *FEAR OF FLYING* A NEW BEST-SELLER. ELIZABETH TAYLOR AND RICHARD BURTON MARRIAGE ON THE ROCKS. HOUSTON FORECASTS TOTAL ECLIPSE OF THE MOON.

Suddenly I remembered how we had all watched the first moon landing on television together, a few years ago. We each had a glass of Coca-Cola The Real Thing, for a toast to Neil Armstrong. Carlos hadn't been born yet: I was the youngest. Nodding off on my father's lap, I could hardly keep my eyes open to take in the grainy satellite pictures, but I could feel the excited beating of his heart, his heart that said, We're on the moon, Ellen. Back in my own bed, I dreamed that my father and I were bounding weightlessly through the moondust, while my mother waved at us anxiously through Apollo 11's porthole. Come back safe and sound, do you hear? In our spacesuits Dad and I soared effortlessly over enormous craters before bouncing down — boinng! — on the surface that had been there for millions of years . . . Do you see this erosion here, Ellen? That's caused by sunspots and meteorites.

I was so proud that my helmet got all fogged up inside: I was the only one Dad could explain this important modern stuff to. He poured a trickle of sand into my gloved hand and told me through his mouthpiece: "This contains a lot of different gases, see? Helium, neon, argon, krypton, and xenon."

I nodded.

"Titanium and zirconium," he continued, picking up a stone, "but strangely enough, no trace of europium."

"There *is* some plagioclase and calcium, though," I answered.

"Well done! All right, we'd better collect some samples, hurry."

We threw ourselves into our work, side

by side, in the pale green light of the moonscape. From time to time we'd beep each other: "A-OK in there, over?" It wasn't until our pockets were bursting with specimens for the scientists in Houston, with their clipboards and white lab coats, that we hopped, skipped, and jumped back to our lunar module in the Sea of Tranquility and signaled to Mama that she could bring us back on board.

After removing our helmets, we dug into a plate of astronaut food, which consisted of colored pills. After that, Dad explained to me what a nanosecond was and that a light-year isn't a measure of time but of distance. "And take that thumb out of your mouth, please."

"But I'm so tired."

"It certainly is a giant leap for mankind," he said. It was such an apt description that it took my breath away: a hundred years from now children would still be coming across that phrase in their history books.

When I woke up in my attic bed, I was the happiest little girl in the whole Milky Way. Everyone had a father, but mine was a hero, a pioneer, a daredevil.

On my way to the bathroom I bumped into him in the corridor and flung my arms around his hips. "Dad," I asked, "so what exactly *is* the difference between krypton and xenon?"

"Oh, sure, and the capital of Iceland is Reykjavík too, little Miss Know-it-all," he groused, shaking himself free of me.

I stood in the middle of the garden in the dismal rain, looking at him seated behind his office window.

My father was a such a jerk. I was pissed off at him.

He was supposed to take care of us — that's what fathers were for — but these days he always seemed to be weaseling out of it: he never sat down to a meal with us anymore; in the evenings he never came to sit in his chair in the sunroom. He was simply never around anymore. He skulked through the house like the Invisible Man. Kes said his impression of wallpaper was absolutely brilliant, but I couldn't find it in me to laugh about it. He was hiding from all of us, behind his desk.

He even slept in his office these days, according to Billie. She'd seen it with her own eyes one night on her way to the kitchen for a midnight snack. The door to his room had been open a crack, and she'd seen his feet hanging over the armrest of the old sofa. He'd still had his socks on.

No wonder, then, that Mama was fed up with him. She was doing her best to hide it from us, but her eyes grew cold and hard when my father's name came up, and she'd purse her lips. My father was supposed to lie in bed beside her; that's what married people did. He was supposed to whisper sweet nothings in her ear and calm her down when she was in one of her moods, yelling at us that we were the devil's own children and a viper's brood. Just think: my own father had no idea what foul insults were being hurled at us. He didn't have an inkling, really, about what was going on in our house. If you encountered him on the stairs, he stared shyly down at his feet and hunched his shoulders, like someone who was unbearably ashamed of himself. As well he should be.

At first I thought it was our fault, or possibly just mine, because I talked too much. Or maybe it was because of my breasts. I should never have bothered him about those, that night when I'd suddenly felt them growing: that had been the turning point, the night when he had turned into wallpaper. My mother's reaction had been equally negative. I asked her the next morning if I could have some money to buy a bra. She'd gone all white and snarled, in her ventriloquist's voice, "Are you starting now, too?"

A little while later, at breakfast, she lashed out at Billie's head with the frying pan because she thought Billie was wearing eye shadow. I was a total basket case. Once I reached school I was sure I'd never have the guts to go home again. I had to do something; I had to think of something. And suddenly I knew what to do. I would simply go to my teacher of ancient Greek and tell her everything. She had a motorbike; I worshiped her. As luck would have it, Greek was my last class of the day.

So after Homer I hung around until everyone had left. As she was sliding her books into her briefcase, I walked up to her desk.

"Anything wrong, Ellen?" she smiled.

"Oh, nothing," I said, nodding my head yes.

She started to laugh, but as I haltingly began my story, her face turned serious. Before long she interrupted me. "Really, Ellen, I don't think your parents will appreciate it if you air their dirty linen in public. You know what I mean by that expression, don't you? Every family has its problems, but that sort of thing is supposed to stay within four walls. Tell me, what's it to do with me that your parents don't sleep together anymore? They wouldn't be at all happy if they knew you had told me. And I wouldn't blame them either, because it really is none of my business."

"But there's other stuff too," I said quickly.

"What am I supposed to do with this sort of information? Really, I'm surprised at you. I always thought of you as such a sensible girl."

I hung my head.

She took my chin in her hand. "Hey, weeping willow. It really isn't the end of the world, you know. There! I've already forgotten what you just told me. And you're probably getting yourself all worked up over nothing. Married couples do sometimes go through difficult times, but you needn't immediately think the worst. Are you afraid they're going to get divorced? Is that it?"

"My little sister's sick all the time, too," I said helplessly. I decided to skip the part about my breasts.

"Yes, and that's probably putting a great strain on everyone, am I right? Know what I think, Ellen? I think that everything will come out all right in the end by itself.

Trust me." She pinched my cheek reassuringly, and man-oh-man, it did cheer me up no end. It's true, I always was such a worrywart. Of course everything would turn out all right by itself.

It wasn't until I was on my bike that the doubts came flooding back. If, like my teacher, you were up to your eyeballs in Greek tragedies all day, in which entire royal dynasties managed to exterminate each other without shedding a tear, then perhaps certain things might seem more ordinary to you than to other people. Woe, woe, the chorus would lament dryly, and that was that. But the bit about not airing our dirty laundry in public was something I did take to heart. Armed with the best of intentions, I rode home in the pouring rain.

Carlos was sitting on the edge of his bed kicking his legs. I quickly attempted to blow-dry my hair with Billie's hair dryer before Mama noticed I was drenched.

"What did you do today?" I asked.

"Nothing," he said listlessly. His beautiful curls were plastered to his face, because of the turtleneck he wouldn't be parted from despite the heat inside the house. He hadn't had a shower in weeks;

Billie and I just couldn't wrestle him out of that shirt. There was a black ring around his neck, and his hands were always grubby. Mama never seemed to notice.

Kes said dirt was good for you when you were three and a half. Only later, he said, it might become a problem. Some day he'd have a talk with Carlos himself, man to man, and together they'd come up with a solution.

"Why don't you go downstairs? You can play a little longer," I urged my little brother.

"Mama's punishing me." He picked at his lip unhappily.

"Have you been naughty?"

He shrugged.

Troubled, I sat down next to him. "You must have been a naughty boy," I said hopefully, "or else you wouldn't be in trouble, would you?"

"I only wanted to change Sophie's diaper. She was so stinky."

"You idiot! You probably stuck her with a safety pin, didn't you! You're much too little to change her! You don't even know how!"

"Yes I do!" He was going all red in the face with indignation. "I dried her whole wee-wee! With a cloth."

I could just picture him at it, with a

frown of concentration, first on his tippy-toes to take a clean diaper from the top bureau drawer, then earnestly bending over the half-naked baby, panting with the effort. Our Carlos, he was such a lamb.

"And then Mama came in, and she . . ." He gasped for air, choking with despair.

"Yes, but, sweetie, Sophie isn't a toy. What if you had hurt her by accident. Or if she —"

At that point my mother called up the stairs that dinner was ready, and I feverishly switched the hair dryer to high.

"Ellen! Michael! What's keeping you?"

Carlos said, astonished, "I'm allowed down to dinner!"

In the kitchen, Mama was putting a casserole on the table. "Hurry, come and sit down, you two. Michael, would you like milk or buttermilk?"

"What's Kes having?" Carlos asked cautiously.

"Milk," said Kester.

"Me too then. If you please."

"Bunch of milkmouths," said Billie.

My mother laughed. "Don't mind her, Michael. Milk makes the man. Just look at Kester."

Kester balled his fist to show off his biceps.

My mother put a glass of milk in front of

him. "And you, little girl of mine?" she asked me.

"I don't care for anything to drink, thank you," I said. God, what a traitor I'd been. See what a warm and happy place our home was after all.

"Well, children," Mama said, sitting down next to Sophie's cradle, "we're ready for a nice meal. I just hope I didn't forget the salt again." She picked up the serving spoon, rested it on the lid of the pan, and glanced from one to the other. We folded our hands. "Sybille, you begin."

Billie was wearing a long-sleeved shirt, buttoned up to the very top. She closed her eyes: "Merciful God." Her voice was unsteady. "Look down upon our little sister with compassion."

Kester followed up in a monotone: "Merciful God, relieve her of all her suffering."

Now it was my turn. But I felt a sneeze coming. I pressed my tongue as hard as I could against the roof of my mouth. Just then my mother said, "Wait, Ellen." She held up her hand with a contemplative look. "It sometimes seems to me as if God isn't even hearing us."

"Oh, but he does listen, Mama," said Billie urgently.

"I think he does too," Kes agreed.

Anxiously my mother looked at me.

My nose was itching and hundreds of germs jostled each other inside my throat, threatening to come flying out of me any moment.

"Ellen?"

Panicked, I shook my head.

Nervously my mother stroked her lips with the tips of her fingers. Suddenly her face lit up. "Know what? I think it might be best if from now on you prayed to me instead. After all, I'm the one taking care of Ida. I believe it is God's will: your prayers will give me the strength to heal her."

"And make her healthy and strong," lisped Carlos.

"Amen," I quickly prompted him, having succeeded in biting back my sneeze.

"You skipped your own part, Ellen. Go on."

I took a deep breath and rounded my shoulders. "Merciful Mama, drive out the evil that's in our little sister."

"Michael?"

"And make her healthy and strong again amen," Carlos rattled off quickly.

"All right, dig in," said my mother.

Billie was staring at me. She really was

an idiot. Couldn't she see that everything was finally beginning to make sense? Only Mama, not God, could free Sophie from evil: and that was by never calling her Ida again, which went for the rest of us too. We ate our stew without salt and for dessert we had vanilla pudding.

Sometimes, when I think of the child I once was, at the mercy of circumstances which I didn't understand but which I was trying with all my might to control, I'd like to take myself in my arms to rock and comfort me and whisper endearments into my ear. Should such an impulse be suppressed or encouraged? I'm still not clear on that.

All the shrinks I went to (and I wore out one after another) after I turned eighteen and moved out of the Unicorn, were of different minds about this. What one called regression the other might diagnose as hysterical conversion, transference, or psychosis. As it turned out, the same symptom could go by many different names. Sometimes, at my wits' end, I would dial Marti's number thinking I'd ask her for advice, but as soon as she answered, I'd hang up, ashamed of my questions, of the fact that I had nobody to consult but her, ashamed of my loneliness.

I was beset by migraine headaches. These came on like thunderstorms, with white streaks of lightning and rolling claps of thunder invading my smallest blood vessels. It got so bad sometimes that in my despair I wanted to saw off my own head.

In those first confusing years when I lived in rented rooms and was always late for my classes, some of the therapists told me that my headaches were self-imposed, an escape from reality. They were also of the opinion that it was my self-destructiveness that made me comb the bars at night and throw myself away like a piece of trash into the first pair of arms that came along. Others considered this a perfectly normal reaction, one I should by all means "act out" because of my need to feel loved. Their kind of therapy usually involved plenty of pillows for kicking and pummeling, preferably in a group session with other traumatized, disturbed, and maddened souls. That was known as group dynamics; we were known as the ultimate authorities on real-life experience.

For a time my problem was an anal-compulsive personality; then it was manic depression. There wasn't a diagnosis that wasn't pinned on me at one time or another; I would lug my new label around with me for a while like a leper clutching his rattle. Sometimes, in the cafeteria or the street, the urge would come over me to announce out loud, "I am Ellen van Bemmel," and I'd be only half convinced of it myself.

One terrible sleepless night, I became totally unhinged, after it hit me that in Italy, Milan was called Milano — and yet they were still one and the same place. Calm down, kiddo, said Kester, we have all the time in the world, we'll sort it out in the end.

What we were after, you see, was the correct term, the one true name, explicit and clear-cut, which would clarify everything and make sense of it all.

We finally found it on a rainy Wednesday morning, during a gynecology lecture. I was halfway through my medical studies.

It was the heyday of what they called the women's movement. You didn't take notes in class; you knitted. Then you huddled together afterward and wrote a manifesto. Wombs and ovaries being removed at the drop of a hat by gynecologists out to make a quick buck; it was an outrage! All that was going to change, my fellow students would see to that.

I did not consider myself one of them. I shared neither their self-assurance nor their opinions, so I remained on the sidelines. I was used to keeping my eyes fixed on the ground. But to this day I can still feel my head suddenly jerking up, my heart missing a good number of beats, my brain going into mental arrest, when our rather progressive professor began discussing postnatal depression, an affliction also known, in its most extreme manifestation, as postpartum psychosis.

"Extravagant mood swings, loss of touch with reality, hallucinations, delusions, paranoid fears and excessive worrying, changes in personality and in behavior, violent intent toward oneself or others," is how she summed up the symptoms. She glanced at her notes. "It is caused by a hormonal imbalance brought on by pregnancy and childbirth. The bottom line is that the patient has no control over her own behavior. Having people tell her impatiently that she should try to pull herself together is therefore useless. The only thing guaranteed to work quickly and effectively is a course of the right medication."

A heated discussion broke out around me. My fellow students wondered indignantly why doctors found it so hard to see womanhood as a natural condition, and therefore women as a class of humans whose natural chemistry could occasionally simply go awry. The medical profession just automatically dismissed the biochemical disorders of childbirth as a load of whining. As soon as you had your baby, you were supposed to be happy and content; if you weren't, you were either a hysteric or a hypochondriac. You could have some Valium, but that was all. As if Valium were of any use when it came to hormonal pandemonium!

I got up and fought my way out of the packed lecture hall. Stunned, I realized that I finally had it, the true name of the mystery that had destroyed our family. Postpartum psychosis. The tragedy need never have happened if my mother's condition had been correctly diagnosed and treated. For years my shrinks had assured me that she must have been completely insane and that she ought to have been locked up in a mental institution. But no matter how out of touch with reality she had been in her disturbed state, I now knew that neither electric shock therapy nor psychoanalysis nor institutionalization could have made her come to her senses. All she had needed was somebody to prescribe the right medication for her. That was the most devastating realization of all.

That same afternoon found me sitting across from shrink number six armed with my notes from the lecture. Shaking, beside myself with fury, I read them out to him. From time to time I had to stop because I was blubbering so much.

He pushed a box of tissues across the desk at me, giving me one of his probing looks. His name was Marco. He believed in calling patients by their first names as a way to promote mutual trust. There was a seashell on his desk, a souvenir from some vacation or other. Whenever he closed up shop, which he could easily afford to do three times a year thanks to our mental distress, the rest of us disturbed, traumatized, and demented souls just had to keep our heads above water as best we could. That was the rule. Before he went skiing or sailing, Marco always insisted on a pact: you had to swear to him you wouldn't commit suicide while he was away.

"If what you now suspect about your mother were true, Ellen," he said slowly, "would that help you to come to terms with the actual history of the thing? Of course that would be an enormous breakthrough."

The actual history? Did he mean *my* history? "What is this, a conspiracy or something?" I yelled suddenly. "I've spent half my life sitting here describing her behavior to you sons of bitches and nobody ever —"

"*You* are my patient, not your mother. And besides, what you've been reading to me is based on rather recent research."

"Recent! Women have been having babies since the year one! Over all those centuries, what became of all the young mothers who had endocrinological problems after childbirth? Did they all end up in the loony bin?"

"Endocrinology didn't exist in the year one. Let's try to work out what this discovery might mean to *you*, shall we? If this can be a starting point for a reconciliation with your mother, then naturally I will do all I can to help you work on it."

"It's an outrage! She should just have been given the right treatment, that's all."

"Not according to the medical and psychiatric practices of the day," he said patiently. "Be reasonable, Ellen. How can something be diagnosed if no one even knows it exists or what it's called? How could your mother's state of mind have been interpreted as a physical illness at a time when it wasn't categorized as such? You just said it yourself: back then, every form of postnatal depression was classified as a psychological complaint, or even a figment of the imagination. Do you really think you can find someone to blame now?"

Of course Marco had personal reasons for having little patience with the idea that insanity might be purely physical in nature. What if that applied to some of his own patients! If they could just get over it by taking a pill three times a day, how would he ever get to the Bahamas again?

I blew my nose into one of his tissues and said, "I don't think I want to make another appointment."

"So you want to run away?" he asked. He leaned back, cocksure. He was only a year or so older than me. There was a good chance he had graduated at the end of my own first year in medical school; he may even have belonged to the society that had once made off with my own club's bar. Pissed out of their tiny minds, eighteen of them had entered our cellar, grabbed hold of our little bar, bent their knees, and, with some primitive grunts, pulled the entire contraption off the floor, so that the beer lines snapped and, to add insult to injury, we found ourselves standing up to our ankles in shattered glass.

"Ellen! You're daydreaming!"

"What were you saying?" It wasn't unusual for me to drift off.

"Why do you suddenly want to run away?" With nicotine-stained fingers, he was playing with the shell on his desk. Marco of the no-suicide pacts was rather fond of a smoke himself.

"Because I don't need you anymore."

"Do you really think that this will cure you? You hear voices; you suffer from —"

"You're the one making an issue of it. Not me."

"Healthy people don't hear voices. I'm telling you, if at this very critical juncture you escape into your delusions, if you let Billie and Kes gain the upper hand now, then I don't think there's much hope you'll —"

"My sister's name is Sybille. My brother is Kester."

"Used to be. They're dead."

"As long as I am alive, they aren't dead. That's no delusion; it's the truth. Anyone who has ever loved someone who isn't there anymore knows it."

"But you've got to get on with your life! You've got to start building up meaningful relationships with an eye to the future, not just the past." He half rose from his seat; I could see the fly of his khakis appearing over the edge of the desk. But instead he intended me to look at his wedding ring, which he was waving at me triumphantly. Look at me, Ellen. I am loved the right way, by the living. With a bit of luck we'll get you there too.

"Pooh," said Billie, and I guffawed out loud.

I looked at my own hands: ringless perhaps, but hands that could cobble together just about anything Kes took it into his head to make. We could, to take just a random example, build a giant catapult and, like medieval warriors, fire a volley of corpses into Marco's office through the window: let *him* try sitting up to his waist in dead bodies for a change.

If you asked me, people just didn't know what they were talking about. They had no idea.

"Well, Marco," I said. "I'm off then."

"Sit down, Ellen. You have serious problems. We have over ten minutes left."

It wasn't as if I couldn't have used a little more serenity and equilibrium in my life —

but not at the expense of renouncing all the love left to me. As I stalked out of the room, I fumbled in my bag for my bike key. "It's in your left pocket," Kes informed me.

Out on the front step, I could spy Marco getting ready for his next customer through the strips of cream-colored blind. He was rolling a cigarette and leafing through a file.

I suddenly felt elated. "What do we do now?" I asked.

"It's nearly time for our internal medicine seminar," Billie said meaningfully. She thought my teacher was to die for. We always went and sat in the front row and tried to catch his attention with our clever questions. He was phenomenal. Actually, most of the gastroenterologists and oncologists were nice people. Their job was to poke around in diseased innards every dismal day, only to discover that the cancer had already spread beyond hope. Contact with their defeated patients had made them soft and pliable, like worn paper. We'd already decided, more or less, that I would go for internal medicine as my specialty.

I hopped onto my bike.

Kes and Billie were jubilant as I left

Marco's street behind me. We'd seen the last of the headshrinkers, and good riddance, too. We should have told him to fuck off long ago. You've got to admit we were right all along, Ellen.

And at last I felt the mysterious throbbing headache, which had followed me from one psychiatrist to the next, starting to lift. Recklessly I lifted my head, spurning my usual focus on pavement, asphalt, and manhole cover. I looked up. A gray, cloudy sky stretched over the city, with a few sparrows here and there. As I rode, I touched my skull, then my temples with my fingers: not an ounce of pain. Gone! The sense of freedom was unbelievable.

"Hey, watch it there," said Billie, "or we'll end up under a streetcar."

I pedaled on, dizzy with relief. So this was what happened when you took fate into your own hands. The moment you started believing in yourself, you were rewarded. No matter what Marco said, I was quite capable of standing on my own two feet. Now that I knew the truth, I never need doubt myself again. All the guilt I had heaped on myself in the Unicorn suddenly melted off my shoulders; all the accusations that I had learned to hurl at my parents in my encounter-group sessions evaporated: none of us had done anything wrong.

Oh, the cruel things I had screeched at my dead mother, foaming at the mouth and stomping viciously on musty cushions! I decided I would go and visit her grave that evening. I finally understood what she was waiting for, beneath that heavy heart-shaped stone. Deep inside the earth she wanted to hear me say, "Mama, I forgive you."

"What is there for *you* to forgive?" Kes promptly asked.

I stopped at a red light, in the nick of time.

"Did *you* get a plastic bag over your head? It's easy for *you* to talk."

"Yes, that's just Ellen all over, isn't it," fumed Billie. "She only ever thinks of herself. Just like Dad."

Dad! It was like being zapped by lightning. Not even I, with the most overactive imagination in the world, could possibly maintain that my father had been suffering from postpartum depression as well.

The light turned green, red again, and then green once more. It was like being under a strobe light at a disco, the traffic racing past me, roaring and blinding, and soon some man, attracted by Billie's charms, would come and take me to his bed, as usual.

I often awoke in unfamiliar, seldom-aired rooms where even the curtains were saturated with the smell of stale Gauloises. The dingy sheets, the plates caked with congealed food scattered all over the floor, and then having to sneak out of there at the crack of dawn, sticky and unwashed, down the creaky stairs and out the front door before some miserable old landlady could read you the riot act; the spare pair of panties in my handbag, the tube of toothpaste I'd lick during my getaway to freshen my breath a little.

I did try to call a halt from time to time, but Billie wouldn't hear of it.

"Hey, are you all right?" In the middle of the noisy street, someone had grabbed me by the arm. A lean young man wheeling a bicycle was staring at me, a concerned frown on his face. "Steady on your feet there!"

I couldn't utter a word.

"Let's go and sit down somewhere for a bit," said Thijs, steering me to the other side. He wasn't Billie's type at all. He was no hunk. More of a weed. He took me to a McDonald's.

At the counter he ordered a cup of

coffee. I asked for a milkshake for Kes, a salad for Billie, and a hamburger for myself. I went and sat down at a little Formica table with Thijs, trying to keep everyone happy. Come on, Kes, I thought you liked strawberry. Billie, look, your favorite.

"Feeling a little better?" asked Thijs.

I took a bite of my hamburger with the bland American cardboard taste, and before I knew it I was telling him about Bureau Van Bemmel. Immediately I could see my father before me, more clearly than I had seen him in years. As I described for Thijs how he used to handle the whole of the U.S. of A., I thought bitterly: fifty federal states plus the District of Columbia under his thumb, but he couldn't protect his own children.

You, Dad, you should have stood up for us! But you didn't lift a finger. The note the police found next to the lifeless bodies said only, *We'll see to it that they don't suffer.* Nothing else. Just that single, unanimous vow. You did it together, and of the two, you were the one who did it in cold blood: *your* hormones weren't all messed up. You sacrificed us to your blind love for a sick, deranged woman. For you, she was the one who always came first. Who says the children of parents who are passionately in

257

love are lucky? Not us! We were in some ways already orphans even when you were still alive. I hope you rot in hell.

"It sounds like you really loved your father, as a child," Thijs said. "You seem so moved. Is he dead, then?"

I rubbed my cold hands together. "He's been dead for years." I thought: All right, Marco, as far as love goes, good luck to you in that department, but you'll never see me try it. Much too dangerous.

"Oh," said Thijs sympathetically, "how . . ."

I said quickly, "But now tell me something about *you*."

He gave a little cough. "I'm an architect. Not that I build anything. I come up with new uses for old, existing buildings." He stirred his coffee with a little plastic stirrer and smiled, his eyes lighting up with enthusiasm. "My trade, you might say, is to do a number on the past."

Billie pursed her lips. "That boy isn't your type, Ellen."

"Let's get out of here," suggested Kes.

Obediently I scrunched up my napkin and began stacking up the containers on my tray.

"Don't you want the rest of your hamburger?" asked Thijs. He pulled the bun toward him and took a bite.

If I ever had to explain to someone how or why Thijs and I got together, I would rewind the reel of our life together back to this fatal moment: his raising my half-eaten hamburger to his lips. The casualness of the gesture, the incredible intimacy of it. As if we were family.

Chewing, he asked, "And you? Do you have a job? Or are you a student?"

"Medicine." Without thinking I snatched the hamburger back from him.

"Aha!" said Thijs, wiping ketchup from the corners of his mouth. "I am sitting across from a lifesaver, or savior, I should say."

"Ha! Say that again," sneered Billie.

"Oh, enough," I begged her. "Can't you just back off for a minute?" I took a bite.

"It's your hamburger," Thijs said, taken aback, "I only thought you didn't want anymore."

I devoured the grilled meat and the soggy bun, thinking I could taste his saliva, as if it were some rare, exotic ingredient.

"Do you want to be a family doctor? Or do you have a specialty in mind?"

"We're going to be a gastroenterologist," said Billie.

"You mean you want to get married to a

gastroenterologist," I snapped at her.

"Well, no, not really," said Thijs. "In my family we don't have too many gastrointestinal problems." He planted his skinny arms on the table and looked at me candidly. "So what would I want with a gastroenterologist?"

And then, as I polished off the last bite, I suddenly realized that I didn't really want to be a doctor at all anymore, not if it meant that someday you might have an enormous mistake on your conscience like the one to which our family owed its tragic end.

"Hey there," said Thijs, "what's the matter?"

He was an architect who didn't build anything: that meant I could be a doctor who didn't cure people. "I'm going to be a pathologist," I said.

I knew I'd hit the bull's-eye. Kes and Billie were bound to be pleased if I chose to be with the dead rather than the living. "Someone who cuts up dead bodies," I explained, for their benefit. The old headache, which had started throbbing again, began to fade a little.

Thijs looked at me with renewed interest. "Well, you certainly are an unusual girl."

"You have no idea how unusual," I replied.

And the rest is, as they say, history.

It has turned hot — typical August weather, close and sweltering, with temperatures that make you long for a good thunderstorm. Fortunately I now have permission from Jan Bramaan to sit up for four hours a day, so at least I can get some fresh air into my lungs at the open window. Not a breath of wind stirs the slats of the blind, which I keep closed almost all the way to keep out the blinding sun. You can smell the hot asphalt of the street. In the distance I can just about make out the sound of hooves from the riding stable where horses amble through the hot sand in sluggish resignation.

The days crawl by in excruciating slow motion, yet I know that elsewhere, people are complaining that there's never enough time. It's as if the clock here has come to a standstill, like at the tea party in *Alice in Wonderland*, and I am the Dormouse, trapped in the same hour for all eternity. But this imposed lethargy is good for Ida-Sophie, and that's the only thing that really counts. For her sake I'd gladly spend three more hot summers immobilized in my chair.

Somewhere in the house Lucia and her children are quarreling. The girls want to go outside, to the pool, the beach. They whine indignantly for ice cream. Then suddenly all three of them shut up.

The sudden silence startles me out of my drowsiness. I listen for the fuss to start up again; instead it remains eerily quiet. At the same moment I see Bas standing at the garden gate with his bike.

He is giving the house a look of appraisal, as if to confirm what he's suspected all along: see, the house is shuttered, all its blinds drawn. Added to the fact that the mail remains unanswered: there's your answer, Ellen must be on vacation. Well, what do you expect, everyone goes away in the summer. His lips move: well done, you were right, Bas. With a complacent expression on his face he walks down the garden path, in a dingy T-shirt with cut-off sleeves, and disappears from my view.

Alarmed, I hoist myself up on the windowsill to follow him through the cracks of the blind. The large clematis next to the front door blocks him from sight. A few moments later he reappears, the green garden hose slung over his shoulder, pushing the lawnmower. Whistling, he couples the hose to the rusty faucet. Then he starts mowing the lawn with energetic lunges.

Tensely I listen to the clattering noise, trying to make myself as small as possible in my chair. He could look up at any time and notice my open window. Then he'd . . . But now I hear the sound of water. He is sprinkling the lawn, lost in the task he's set himself. He was never very good at doing more than one thing at a time.

I inhale the fresh smell of cut grass.

*Don't you mind going to all this trouble, Bas?*

*No, actually, Ellen, I love every minute of it.*

What's he thinking? Why did he send me that postcard? What did he need to speak to me about so urgently?

Cautiously I crane forward again, to catch a glimpse of him.

He is done. With his back to me he coils up the hose, taking his time, his ponytail half stuffed inside his shirt collar as usual. Now he'll amble around to the back to do his watering and mowing there. While Lucia and her brood are probably cowering under the kitchen table with bated breath, their arms wrapped around their knees, heads anxiously pressed together.

Years ago, Kester taught me how to stalk like an American Indian: first you focus on the soles of your feet, next on the little twigs under them that could snap and give you away. Then three minutes of standing on tiptoe, to practice feeling weightless. It was pretty hard to do, but that was the whole point.

I could leave my room right now without making a sound, softly pad through the quiet house, and sneak outside unnoticed. All I'd have to do is concentrate on the soles of my feet, and I'd soon find myself standing behind Bas and tapping him gently on the shoulder. I'd see his face crack into a smile. Hey, Ellen. I thought you'd . . .

I don't deserve his boundless devotion. He'll come to that conclusion himself some day, you'll see. I have a cramp in my calves, I want to rush out of my tepee, I want to explain, I want to make amends before he disappears and goes back to his little roof terrace and his potted geraniums.

"Do you really want to lose Ida-Sophie, then?" Billie intrudes snidely. "You know you're not allowed to walk that far yet."

In spite of the heat, I shiver at the thought. No, I'm not going anywhere.

We remain motionless.

Behind the house, Bas is working away. I assume he's cheerfully talking to himself while doing so. "Should have thought of this earlier. And tomorrow I'll come and weed the flower beds. Ellen will be so surprised when she gets home."

"Ellen. Ellen!" Lucia whispers urgently.

With some difficulty I focus my eyes on her. She is standing in the doorway, flushed and rattled. "There was a man in the garden . . . Has he gone yet?"

"Yes."

"Was it that friend of yours?"

I sit up. "Yes. Didn't I tell you he'd come around sooner or later?"

"Lucky you, to have someone like that."

"You're right; it just goes to show once again that I have everything and you have nothing."

She looks at me blankly.

Suddenly I explode. "Let's stop pussyfooting around, all right? You think I'm just the luckiest person alive, don't you? If I told you what I've —" Appalled, I clamp my jaw shut. She'll never wheedle it out of me.

"Why don't you shut up for once, bitch!" She spits it out, right in my face. "All I was trying to say is, you're lucky to have a friend like that. Is that any reason to yell at me?" She lurches into the room. "You really are a case, aren't you!" She starts tidying up at random, picking up a towel here, slapping at an imaginary speck of dust there. "I've had it up to here with your hysterical nonsense, do you hear?"

"That's lucky." I'm so riled I can hardly get the words out. "Because you'll soon be rid of me, won't you. Just a couple of weeks more and you can simply pull the door shut behind you. Good-bye, old thing, cheerio, good riddance. So — where did you say you were off to, then?"

She freezes, bent over a baseboard.

"Surely you've made plans."

As she straightens up, tears glisten in her eyes. "No! No! I haven't made any plans yet, dammit! I don't know! Happy now?"

She seems so helpless that my anger evaporates. I say flatly, "Oh well, there's plenty of time yet."

She gathers up the newspapers and magazines scattered around my bed. From the set of her shoulders I can see she's crying. "Jesus, Lucia, don't take everything so hard."

"Look who's talking." She takes a handkerchief from her sleeve and blows her nose. "I just don't understand why you always have to act so hateful."

"Well, I . . ." But I can find no words to justify my behavior. What makes me think

I'm any better than Lucia, so docilely re-signed to being the victim? Aren't I just as much a prisoner of . . .

"You really don't need to justify any-thing to her," says Billie.

"Only to us," says Kes. "And don't you forget it."

"Sorry," I mutter.

Lucia throws me a timid, forgiving smile. "Well, I'm not always the easiest person to live with either. Shall I make you some iced tea? Or would you rather have some fresh fruit? I'll go and fetch you a piece of melon."

I feel guilty. I want to call her back. But then Ida-Sophie pokes me hard in one of my ribs with her elbow, as if now it's her turn to pick a bone with me.

Sighing, I put my hands on my stomach. Ida-Sophie, little Ida-Sophie. What do you want from me? My undivided attention? You already have it. You'll always come first, you know that.

Sometimes it worries me, the idea of a child half of whose genetic make-up is a mystery to me, and I wonder what's down the road for us. In my mind I often ex-amine her toes, fingertips, or earlobes, comparing them with my own. Or I'll study the lines in her palms: the left shows the future; the right shows the present –– a clean slate for now.

And where, in what fold of skin, does her past lie hidden? Shall I find traces of the bone-marrow tap she had when they thought she might have leukemia? Where will I uncover the hours she spent under X-ray machines, because of all those inexplicable fractures? Will there be any traces of the internal hemorrhages that came next, the inflamed rashes, the diarrhea?

The last picture of her in my album is a portrait, taken up close, harshly lit with a flashbulb. There is precious little left of the lively baby she had been, after her recovery from the intestinal blockage. In the bony little face her eyes peek out listlessly; her nose is sunken and leprous; there are just a few wispy tufts of hair left.

Kes took that snapshot. He had just bought his telephoto lens, after months of saving up for it.

I'm making funny faces, but at the same time I make sure to keep one eye on the French doors and the other on the candle and the incense next to Sophie's crib: to-night it's my turn to keep watch. My mother is in the kitchen, testing Billie on her biology. They're up to the vertebrates.

"And now one without crossing your eyes, Ellen," says Kester.

"No, take one of Sophie now."

"Take one of Sophie's arm," cries Carlos, "like at the doctor's!"

"As long as the flash doesn't wake her up," says Kes.

"You can take it from a distance, can't you, with that lens? Go on. For Mama. We'll put it in a nice frame for her."

Kester mutters something under his breath. He can't stand the fact that I'm always coming up with the best ideas. But I can't help it, can I? I look in the crib to see if Sophie is looking presentable. Her breath comes in short rasps. Carefully I smooth a wisp of hair over the bruise on her temple. I pull the blanket up to her chin. I don't want the plaster cast to show in the picture.

Kester fiddles with the camera settings, muttering numbers under his breath. It takes ages. Finally he takes a shot. "Another one, just to make sure," he says, coming a few steps closer. "Just move away from that crib, go on."

I go and sit on the wicker loveseat, next to Carlos. "You're up much too close. You should . . ." I spin around because I hear the door open.

It's my father.

I stare at him in consternation. Mr. Invisible himself.

He shuts the door carefully behind him. Then he says formally, "Well then, young ladies and gentlemen." He works his mouth from side to side. He sticks his hands into his pants pockets, takes them out again, and looks around as if he isn't certain if he can just go and sit down anywhere. There is a long-drawn-out silence, the only noise the creaking of the loveseat as Carlos wriggles off. He runs to Dad on his short little legs. "I've had three glasses of milk!"

"Well now, I can see that." He picks Carlos up. "If you keep this up, you're going to be a giant. You're already almost too heavy for me." Then he glances quickly from Kes to me. "And how are things otherwise around here?"

Kester mutely twiddles the rings of his new lens. I hear them clicking softly. Don't you think Dad does a brilliant wallpaper impression, Ellen? That's Kes for you: he can sulk like a mule. So we're invisible to

Dad, are we? Then so is he to us. Don't think you can make it up to us by sucking up to us now, the way you can with Carlos. We have our principles.

"Cat got your tongues?" my father asks with forced jollity. Carlos is climbing up onto his shoulders. He is squealing with delight.

Kester runs his fingers through his hair. He's at least as cool-looking as Billie, even if he doesn't know it himself. I suspect he spends the stolen moments he calls his "privacy" secretly steaming his face over the sink, to get rid of the blackheads. If you ask me, even Elvis would be jealous if he saw him. I've got to remember to tell him later.

"Look, Dad, I have a telephoto lens," he suddenly blurts out in his squeaky voice. "It fits your camera, but of course I'm saving up for my own one now." He simpers, with a shy, lopsided grin.

"My goodness, what a purchase. What ASA have you got there?"

"A hundred," says Kes eagerly.

"Then your pictures will turn out splendidly, I'm sure."

Envy and fury churn into a nauseating lump in my stomach. If I'm not careful, I'll burst into tears. You're such a crybaby,

271

Ellen. Do you really have to blubber at every little thing? "You stupid clod," I yell at Kester. "It's two hundred ASA. It's Dad's camera and it's Dad's roll of film. You haven't got a clue!"

My father lowers Carlos to the ground and sits down next to me. There's at least a foot and a half between us. I pull up my knees and wrap my arms around them.

"I wanted to have a little word with all of you." He turns to face me.

The fact that he hasn't shaved fills me with revulsion. I can see hairs growing out of his nose; they're right there in my line of sight. I wiggle from one buttock to the other. "You've come to tell us that you're going to divorce Mama, I suppose," I say angrily. "And that you're going to live somewhere else."

Carlos flops down next to Dad. "Why?" he asks, his eyes round as saucers.

Kester keeps quiet. His face is red as a beet. He stands in the middle of the sun-room, rooted to the floor.

"Whatever gave you that idea, Ellen?" my father asks. He rubs his chin uncertainly. "You really need never worry that I . . . that I would . . . Your mother and you, no, I'd never . . ."

It makes my blood boil. I don't want a

father who hems and haws. I want one who comes right out and says it, a father whose every word doesn't need to be painfully dragged out of him. "Why do you sleep in the office then?" I hurl at him.

He tries to laugh. "You don't miss a thing, do you."

"And in the daytime too, you stay in your office even when we're eating!"

"Yes, but it's because . . . See, well, it's true that Mama and I . . . we had a fight, but it's all going to sort itself out, don't you worry about that. I've just been trying to stay out of her way as much as possible for the moment, so that things can simmer down a little. Do you understand? She's on such a short fuse these days. She's so . . ."

He looks at me imploringly. Don't you think so, Ellen?

Tattletale, ratfink. A good thing you won't find *me* airing our dirty linen. I fix my gaze on the potted tree in the corner. Principles give you something to hold on to.

"My little girl." He sticks out a hand. "Come here a minute."

I wiggle my toes inside my shoes. I can't stand this. "So what did you want to talk to us about, then?" I snap.

He pulls his hand back and says, "To be

quite honest, I'm rather worried about Mama. She's not herself, I'm afraid. I may be wrong, of course, I know I have rather kept to myself, these past weeks. But I did want to find out what you think of it."

"What we think of what?" I ask.

My father coughs. "She isn't . . . mean to you, is she?"

Kester looks at the ceiling.

Carlos has found a piece of Lego under the loveseat and twiddles it in his fingers. His mouth is hanging open. He looks retarded.

"You do know, don't you, that you can always come to me if there's anything wrong?" my father asks.

I jerk my head around and glare at him. "Not true. Your door's closed all day."

"I've just explained it to you, haven't I? But perhaps, yes, by God, Ellen, perhaps that's not the way to make things better. Perhaps Mama and I should just . . . if we went away for a few weeks . . . if the two of us took a holiday, then . . ."

"Me too," says Carlos. He is tugging anxiously at my father's sleeve.

"She'll never go," I sneer. "Do you really think she'll leave Sophie to go and sit on a beach somewhere with you?"

My father gets up and walks over to the

274

crib. His knees buckle briefly. "That fracture will heal by itself; she doesn't need Mama for that."

"Sure, *this* fracture! But then she'll have another one!" Mama always says that our little sister only needs to wave her little arm to break her wrist. It's rare in a baby, such a fragile little frame: the doctors can't figure it out either. The only thing doctors are good for is setting the bones once they're already broken.

"You don't get it, do you," I blurt out. "You just sit at your desk, while we —"

"All right, that's enough, Ellen!"

Seething with indignation, I jump up and run out of the room before that sadist can clock me one. I take the stairs three steps at a time. In the attic I dig out my diary and scribble it all down, in one fell swoop: my father is a useless piece of shit, that's all there is to it. He might just as well not be there at all.

My cheeks are on fire, and when I've spilled my guts out, I lean out of the dormer window to cool off a bit. It's a cloudy, windy evening. Every now and then a little pockmarked slice of moon peeks out from behind the clouds, but never for long. The ancient Greeks used to think that's where the Elysian fields were, on the moon; that's where you went when you died. I flop back down on my bed and scrawl in large angry letters in my diary: *GO TO THE MOON. GO TO HELL.* And suddenly tears fill my eyes.

How many moon landings ago was it that I sat on my father's lap watching Apollo 11? NASA is already up to its sixteenth or seventeenth Apollo by now. I don't get it, why do those people in Houston still bother? After all, the moon is definitely uninhabited; Dad and I saw it with our own eyes. It's cold there, and dark, and inhospitable.

# Michael and his Lego castle, 31 March 1973

I visited my brother Carlos just once, when he turned five. I hadn't seen him in almost a year. In the beginning, I used to talk to him regularly: Marti phoned the Kamphuis family for a little chat once every other week, and then they'd put Carlos on the line. Marti would leave me alone for a few minutes in her office. She knew she could trust me.

Leaning against the steel desk where Carlos and I used to produce drawings for her, I'd wait impatiently for my little brother. I had a thousand things to ask him and to tell him. I'd been looking forward to our chat for two interminable weeks; on my calendar, every second and fourth Sunday of the month was marked with a little red heart with an arrow through it. I often could think of nothing else.

My longing stuck in my throat like a fishbone: I would cough my guts out while waiting for him to come to the phone. I was simply dying to hear one of his familiar *whys;* I wanted to spend at least ten minutes smacking kisses down the receiver.

His clear little voice, in my ear, sounded surprised. "Ellen?"

"You idiot," I snarled, instantly hurt, "who'd you expect? I always phone at this time! Why do I bother!"

He didn't react. "I'm allowed to stay up late tonight."

"Well, then you'll just be nice and grouchy tomorrow, won't you? You dummy, you've *got* to go to bed on time. Do you hear me?"

"Not true! I'm allowed —"

"Otherwise you'll be whimpering and whining all day, like you always do, you're such a baby."

It was always the same. No matter how I swore to myself I wouldn't, I just couldn't help myself: hurtful words would just roll out of my mouth, just as my hands had once independently shredded half a year's worth of Henry Kissinger. I could never manage to bring out "Charlie, I miss you so much." Maybe that meant I didn't really miss him after all.

Which was why I hollowly informed Marti, after a while, that I didn't need to talk to him on the phone anymore.

She thought I was an ungrateful little

brat. It was so nice of Mr. and Mrs. Kamphuis to permit us to keep in touch. It showed they had my brother's best interests at heart, and mine as well. And wasn't I interested in knowing how he was doing?

I already knew how he was doing. "He has two hamsters and a train with a real steam engine," I rattled off. "And under his bed, which you get to by climbing up a little ladder, there's a blue toy chest, just for him and no one else. And on Sundays they have pancakes."

"My, my, then you must envy Michael sometimes."

"His name's Carlos! And Sunday is for *fish*cakes!" I was seething. That they could get away with it, messing with the way things were supposed to be, just because they felt like it.

I crossed out all the little hearts on the calendar; I scratched them out with a marker until they turned into black holes. The first thing I saw on waking up in the morning was that mangy thing hanging there. Marlies had given it to me when she still thought we were friends. What was the point of having a calendar with pictures of ponies on it? I didn't have anyone whose birthday I needed to remember. I tossed it into the wastebasket, opened my Livy, and immersed myself blindly in his endless numbers of cohorts.

I studied like a maniac: at least it kept my mind occupied, all those soldiers marching through my head, on their way to victory or to defeat, Livy didn't care which. All he did was write it down and record it. Woe, woe, wasn't something you ever heard him say.

Time didn't exactly fly. It was a slow, obstinate succession of day following night, night following day. I couldn't say I was happy.

Then a letter arrived.

I had had just one piece of mail since I'd been at the Unicorn. Bas's tulip field, however, had already started to fade over my bed, as if he, the only living person I still knew from my youth, was now also on the point of crossing over into the underworld. Still, the letter could only be from him. It took me three days to open it, as if I could prolong Bas's life that way. Finally my curiosity got the better of me.

She had signed the letter, *Mother Kamphuis.*

Marti said I had to go, and no further discussion. She gave me some money to buy Carlos a present, and for the train ticket.

I bought a stuffed dog named Toby and then went to the station — Haarlem Station, the one Carlos and I hadn't been able to find on Christmas Eve. How terribly cold it had been that night. The endless slogging through the frozen, deserted streets. The way my old headmaster had informed me my brother couldn't hide out at his place. You really couldn't count on anybody, ever.

There they were on the platform at Beverwijk waiting for me, the three of them.

"Well! This *is* nice, Ellen," said Mother Kamphuis. She still had the gray bun. Shyly I offered her my hand.

"Go on, give your little brother a big hug now."

Carlos was wearing a new jacket. He had grown taller, and he didn't have his baby curls anymore. He kept his hands behind his back. I couldn't make myself give him a kiss.

"We all have to get used to each other a little first," said Father Kamphuis diplomatically.

They lived close to the railway station in a small squat house with no front yard. There was a beige three-piece living-room set and a gleaming wall unit with glass doors. I'd never been inside a house like this. I felt large and fat in it, as if in stepping over the threshold I had suddenly grown several inches in every direction.

One of the dining-room chairs was festooned with streamers. That was for Carlos. Father and Mother Kamphuis bustled about, talking to each other under their breath. They poured a glass of soda for each of us: it wasn't even The Real Thing; it was Pepsi. They brought out a huge chocolate cake with five candles on it which my brother had to blow out after they had sung "Happy Birthday to You" in warbly voices. Then they cut the cake. Isn't this nice? Will you? Or shall I? Oh, wait a minute.

I munched my slice of cake as slowly as possible, because you can't be expected to talk with your mouth full.

Carlos was wearing a sweatshirt without a turtleneck.

"I bet Ellen would like to have a look at your presents," said Mother Kamphuis, giving me a prodding look. "Wouldn't you, Ellen?" She nodded at the wrapped package I hadn't yet handed over. I quickly pulled it closer to me.

Father Kamphuis cleared his throat.

"What do you do for a living?" I asked,

relieved to have finally thought of a topic of conversation.

He looked at me in astonishment. "I'm an accountant."

"That must be rather boring," I remarked politely.

Mother Kamphuis snickered and tried to turn it into a cough. "You must be curious to see your little brother's room. Why don't you go up and have a look, both of you?"

I followed Carlos up the stairs. He didn't scramble up on all fours anymore. It really shocked me, the way he'd just gone on growing up without me.

In his room he climbed just as sure-footedly up the ladder to his bunk bed. So it was true about the bed. It blew me away. Since he didn't say anything, I just went and sat down underneath it, on the blue chest, gazing at his dangling feet. He was wearing Donald Duck socks.

Next I spent some time admiring his hamsters, which were huddled together in a glass tank filled with wood-shavings, asleep. I didn't spot the train my brother had bragged about so much, though. There were drawings pinned on the wall. And from the looks of it, he could now do much more than just coloring in. I wondered if he'd had any skin grafts yet. Maybe they would let him go once they had paid for all the operations. That was the reason they'd taken him from me in the first place, wasn't it? He hadn't even put up a struggle; he had just let them take him. He should have just run away again! Had he forgotten that he belonged with me? After all I'd done for him? What was he thinking? And suddenly I knew the answer, painful as it was. My brother thought he was Michael Kamphuis.

My entire body rebelled at the thought; I almost threw up right then and there. I was the cement, but I had failed. Carlos's name would never be added to the list on the heart of stone, the heart beneath which we were so longingly awaited. Only my name would be chiseled on there. Already I could see the sparks flying; I could hear the clanging of iron on steel and smell the prickly dryness of the flying dust. But it wasn't good enough.

Carlos was dead, even deader than the rest of my family.

I got up. One of my legs had fallen asleep, and I almost fell over. In the middle of the room I hesitated, in a daze. I couldn't decide whether to turn around or not. I had no idea what would happen if I saw him sitting on his bed. And what was he thinking, all this time? What would he do if I . . . what, if I what?

He was sitting bolt upright, staring at me with a wary expression on his face. He was hugging a huge stuffed Dalmatian, fondling it absently. He didn't need my Toby at all.

And then I suddenly saw the fine red lines around his neck. They had already sewn new pieces of skin on. Whenever I complained of being too big or too little, too fat or too thin, my mother always used to say, "Too bad, Ellen, but you know I can't put you back in the oven and bake you over again." But that's exactly what they were doing with Carlos. They hadn't just given him a new name; they were also giving him a new exterior.

I started backing away, until I bumped into the door behind me.

On top of his bed, in his room so full of lovely things specially bought for him, Michael Kamphuis was hugging his cuddly toy, as if he couldn't care less about anything else. Then he picked up a picture book and began leafing through it, as if totally engrossed.

It wasn't until I reached the stairs that I began to cry. Blinded by tears I stumbled downstairs, grabbed my coat from the rack, and slipped out of the house. We hadn't exchanged a word, not one single word.

I still regret that I went straight to my room when I got back and ripped his photo from the wall, tearing it into a thousand enraged, tormented snippets. It showed Carlos grinning widely under a rakish cap, a gift from Sjaak. It was such a cute picture.

This one was taken earlier. Here we have Carlos with his Legos. He has built a castle. Beaming with cautious pride, he looks up at my mother, who is standing beside him. She has a happy, carefree expression on her face. It's the last photo in my album.

Seeing her this way, you can't help thinking there's been a miracle: there is a twinkle in her eye; she seems to be the way she always was — our cheerful, down-to-earth mother.

It happened suddenly, out of the blue, as befits a real miracle, which was why it felt so real and convincing: we came home from school one afternoon to find her crafting little Easter chicks out of cotton balls, wire, and crepe paper. "You're going to crack up when you see my Easter bunny," she told us gaily.

It felt so normal to see her occupied like this that it took an hour, the time I spent working on Pythagoras's theorem, for it to hit me how unusual this was nowadays. I crept downstairs and observed her through the crack in the kitchen door. It felt funny, spying on my mother like that.

She and Carlos were sitting at the kitchen table, chatting away, cutting little beaks out of red cardboard with scissors. Charlie's round face was gleaming with pleasure. Sophie was whimpering in her crib, but my mother wasn't paying any attention. "Oh my, what a good job you're doing, honey," she said to my brother.

I had almost forgotten how much I loved her.

We didn't discuss it among ourselves. We all tiptoed through the house, afraid we'd do something that would upset the apple-cart. What had happened? What could have made the tide turn? But with the passing of each new day, the answer became less important. She never spoke in her ventriloquist voice. We didn't hear her mention God or Beelzebub anymore either. She cooked great quantities of Kester's favorite noodle soup. He was working on inventing a four-sided circle, and he could use something to keep his energy up, she said. She showed Carlos and me how to make a human pyramid. Billie was allowed to wear her normal clothes again. She sometimes left Sophie alone for over an hour. She brought my father cups of coffee in the office.

Everyone said she looked wonderful. Esmée, Marie-Louise, Bas — everyone thought so.

I was happy that I'd managed to keep our dirty linen within four walls. I felt like singing all day long. It was only when my mother leaned over Sophie's crib that the old fear would grip me again. I'd watch her like a hawk, but I was worrying over nothing. Sophie was the picture of blazing health. Suddenly there were no more fractures, or any other inexplicable ailments. At dinner we no longer had to pray, "Merciful Mama, make our sister healthy and strong."

Our prayers had been answered, quietly and awesomely.

It made perfect sense, then, that life should suddenly return to normal. I wasn't even really sure if there had ever been anything amiss. When it came right down to it, nobody else had noticed a thing.

In the morning, at breakfast, I'd sometimes smell Mama's funny smell, and Dad
was having meals with us again. I could see,
in the way he'd playfully tweak her fingers
when passing the salt, how happy he was.
How pleased he must be that she allowed
him to scrub the soup pot again, or to help
her fold the sheets. They'd stand facing
each other, each one holding one end of the
sheet, and then pulling it taut with a snap.
You had to do it that way because the
sheets always came out of the laundry lopsided. It always ended with one of them
pretending to be pulled off his or her feet.

At first my father was even more on his
guard than the rest of us. But Mama didn't
shy away anymore when he caressed her
cheek in passing, or when he casually
cupped a hand around her bottom when
he thought we weren't looking.

She sewed a button on his shirt without
making him take it off first. Sitting on his
lap, brandishing a needle and thread, she
asked, "Is there anything else I can help
you with?"

We'd sometimes get that annoying
feeling again that they were behaving like
teenagers.

Billie said, "Oh God, it's going to lead to
another baby."

Kes said, "Might as well start putting the water on to boil."

I asked my father about it. And also if Orson could come back into the house.

Eyes twinkling, he started by blowing his nose elaborately.

"You're making fun of me!"

"On the contrary, sweetheart." He adjusted my collar. "Isn't it about time we bought you a new blouse?"

On Saturday afternoon we went together to the V&D department store in Haarlem; I was allowed to ride there on the back of his bike. He bought me a white shirt with gold butterflies, and for Mama a bottle of perfume. I wondered if the perfume had been the real reason for our going into town.

When we came home Mama said he shouldn't spend his hard-earned money on frippery for her. He laughed. He said he had plenty of other things in mind for her as well. He acted excited and elated.

My mother said teasingly that he looked like someone who was on the point of doing something reckless.

"That isn't like you at all, Dad," said Billie sourly.

He replied, "Oh, but there you're wrong. I would commit murder for your mother if I had to."

The crocuses were already poking out of the ground, blackbirds sang their hearts out early in the morning, and I was beginning to give serious thought to my upcoming birthday. I wanted the single "Dracula" by ZZ & De Maskers, a bottle of patchouli oil, an Afghan coat, and a copy of *Daily Life in Ancient Greece*.

Then the weather changed. April came, and it turned wintry, cold, and nasty. We had to get our sweaters out again. In the afternoon, after delivering the packages to the post office, Kes and I would come home drenched and chilled to the bone. Everyone at Bureau Van Bemmel was walking around sneezing. And then one afternoon, my mother announced, "All right, it's time."

"What do you mean?" I asked. I was alone with her in the kitchen. She was peeling pears; I was peeling potatoes. The light was on.

"I mean that it's time for your vitamins, darling." She sounded calm, but when I looked up, I could see resignation written in her face, and also a fierce sadness.

My mother was not a conventional beauty. She did have good skin, and her inky hair was always shiny, but her features were quite a bit less symmetrical than those of my Greek teacher: her lips just a bit too full, her nose just a touch crooked, her eyes just a little too deep-set. It was a face that had to be animated to be attractive. And yet, in that moment of quiet sadness, she looked more beautiful to me than I'd ever seen her.

Softly she said, "We love you so very very much."

"Come on, don't worry about us, Mama! We won't get sick."

"No, not if you take your vitamins." She was still bathed in the light of that unearthly beauty, a lonely kind of glow. She looked down at her hands. Then she said, "We will see to it that you don't suffer."

The thought that one of her old moods might be coming back made me break into a cold sweat. "OK, then we'll just take twice as many vitamins as you think we need."

Her mouth was smiling, but her eyes remained dull, as if something was hurting her badly. "Good idea, Ellen. I'll go and get them right now."

I started peeling another potato, but my hands were shaking; I couldn't manage an unbroken corkscrew curl.

She came back with a couple of little bottles. Silently she took two blue bowls down from the cupboard and dumped the pills out into them. Placing them on the table in front of me, she said, "Come over here, my big girl."

Before I knew it, I was sitting on her lap. She had washed her hair that morning; it was crackling with static electricity. It tickled my ears and made me giggle in spite of myself.

"Ellen," she said, "now, how are we going to do this?"

"We'll divide them up, a saucer for each." To me it was as simple as ABC. If this was about giving her some peace of mind, we would all swallow a whole soup bowl of vitamins if we had to. "And we'll serve them with the poached pears."

"Really, you think so?" She was relieved; I could hear it in her voice.

I jumped up to take out five saucers.

"Don't forget one for Dad and one for me," she said.

I scurried back to the cupboard.

"Come here, just another little cuddle," she said.

I went to sit on her lap again and leaned against her. She had gained some weight since Sophie's birth; she was nice and soft. With her index finger she stirred the pills in the two bowls. First one, then the other.

"These are the pills Sybille picked up from the pharmacy a while ago, remember? That idiot doctor prescribed them for me. So you see, for everything there is a reason." She sighed. "What we were thinking was two of each. But you think four of each is better, then? I hope we have enough."

She began counting out the pills. White tablets and capsules the color of sand that made me think of the Apollo 11 astronauts' food. How bouncy we'd be after taking those pills; we'd be indestructible! Mama wouldn't have to worry about us anymore.

Lucia is ready and waiting in the entry hall with her paltry luggage when Jan Bramaan buzzes. One short, one long ring of the doorbell.

"All right, then," he says, glancing quickly from her to me. "Is everyone ready?"

For months I've been living for this moment. At last the house is to be mine, all mine again. But there's none of the wild elation I thought I'd feel. That's what happens if you look forward to something too much.

The little girls are sitting, with sullen faces, on the stairs. They don't want to go to a flat in Hoofddorp. Samantha has tears in her eyes.

"Well, I guess we'll be going," says Lucia.

"Yes," I concur. "So — thanks for everything, I guess. Good luck in your new life and all that."

"Thank you, too."

All these formalities. Saying good-bye is not exactly my strong suit. Come on, just get moving, Lucia. Did you pack Vanessa's retainer, or is it still lying around here somewhere?

"I really mean it," she says slowly. "Because if you hadn't been so insufferable, if you hadn't gone on about my future plans in such a nasty, tactless way, I might still be thinking that always being on the run is a perfectly normal way to live." She puts out her hand. Not for me to shake; no, for me to notice that her finger is missing a wedding ring: Lucia has untied the knot. With the help of a social worker she has filed for divorce. She's been boring the pants off me about it for the last few weeks.

Thanks to me, her children no longer have a father. I bend down and pat little

Rochelle's head; she has a green bubble of snot hanging from her nose.

"I *would* like to beat the rush hour, ladies," says Bramaan.

I can hardly be expected to kiss Lucia good-bye.

"I'll give you a ring some time," she says.

"You do that, and I'll tell you you have the wrong number."

"Oh, you're incorrigible!" She flings her arms around me in an impetuous bear hug.

Jan Braaman says, "I'll go and load up the luggage."

Little hands clutch at my legs, my fat stomach. Squashed between Lucia and her kids I almost break down. Before they arrived, this house was a mausoleum. And once their warm bodies have gone and I don't hear any voices around the house anymore . . .

"Ellen is a crybaby," taunts Billie.

"Always a wet hankie," says Kes.

"Oh fuck off," I snap desperately.

Lucia lets go. She says, "My God, I miss your delightful company already."

And off she goes. Really, she's leaving. To start a new life. The little girls trudge after her, their shoulders drooping. Only Samantha stops briefly on the garden path to wave at me.

What do I care? I go inside and make myself a pot of mint tea. I have an almost uncontrollable craving for a cigarette. Instead I eat half a bag of cookies. Then I go outside and sit on the terrace, in the shade. It is still very hot. The hydrangeas hang their heads. I could give Bas a ring, I suppose.

I take out the phone book and open it. Before I know it, he'll pop out from behind the seven digits at the top left-hand corner of the page, in his red jacket, in the information booth. "InterGarden, how may I help you?" he'll say. And then I'll say, "Bas? Is this a bad time? It's Ellen." I still have to thank him for the trouble he's taken with my garden. Good manners never killed anyone.

"InterGarden, how may I help you?" It's a woman's voice.

I hesitate. But what am I afraid of? It's not as if Billie and Kes will give me a hard time about poor Bas. They never did.

"May I speak to Bas Veerman?"

"One moment please."

He's part of our past, after all; he's safe; he belongs to us; there's nothing he can find out about us that he doesn't already know. Thijs was always busy pumping me, year in and year out; he had the patience of

297

a saint; he had to know every little detail. Someone who wasn't there will keep asking questions, questions, questions, until it drives you crazy. Bas will never subject me to a single painful question.

"Veerman speaking."

I grip the receiver firmly. "It's Ellen," I manage.

"Hello! You're back!" I can hear the delight in his voice. "Did you have a nice holiday?"

"Yes, thank you. You've been here, haven't you? The garden looks great." How awkward I sound, like a bashful child.

"No trouble. I was going to plant your flower beds, but I didn't know what you wanted. Shall I come around this evening with some seed? As long as we water it thoroughly, it isn't too late."

Funny how things don't have to be as complicated as you think. I'm really not as antisocial as Lucia seems to think I am. "Sure, I'd love that. I was thinking lupines, and some nasturtiums, and . . ."

"I'll bring an assortment. I'll be there after six."

After hanging up I remain immobile for several minutes, worried that I can feel a headache coming on.

Finally I get up and go to the kitchen.

This is where I found Billie and Kes that night, with plastic bags over their heads fastened around their necks with elastic. They were sitting sort of slumped over at the kitchen table, the saucers that had contained the pills I had prepared for them in front of them. Billie had orange nail polish on.

Oh, Billie! Billie with her freckled chest, the little transistor radio she listened to at night, the cheap doctor romances about blond nurses who always found happiness in the end, her shaved armpits and her padded bras: forever sixteen, cheated of all her plans and all her dreams. What else could I do but open my house and heart to her unconditionally, and give her a room with cotton balls on the floor and movie stars on the walls — sixteen forever?

"Yeah, wow, you really kill me, girl," she teases me. But that flippant tone is all show. For my sister, with all her zest for life, can never just decide one day, as Lucia has decided, that she's had enough of being a victim. She can't take matters into her own hands and start a new life. Actually, she can't do a thing anymore. Nor is resting in peace an option, either, for her or for Kester, as long as I'm still alive. They're condemned to live on inside my head, with even less freedom than I had during my weeks of ordered bed rest. I am responsible for them both; I wouldn't want to have it any other way, and I'll just have to put up with their moods from time to time.

On the counter lies our IKEA catalogue. Look, Billie, there are the curtains I was thinking of. And what do you think, Kes, of this halogen lamp?

That fateful evening, I'd left the table just before dessert because Orson had started howling in his pen. He was standing on his hind legs waiting for me, going crazy. I gave him his food, but that wasn't what he wanted. He just kept making a mad racket and jumping up on me. Finally, not knowing what else to do, I grabbed his leash and took him out for a long walk.

When I returned, over an hour later, I could see my parents silhouetted in the sunroom. The light wasn't on, but I didn't need it to make out the scene. My father was taking a little nap on the sofa, as he often did after supper. My mother was sitting by him. She was holding his hand; his head was on her lap. I started to whistle as I walked to the kitchen. We qualified for an Oscar, I decided. An Oscar for Best

Family. On TV, Dennis Hopper would descend the glittering staircase in his *Easy Rider* boots and read out our name. The whole world would break into applause.

In the kitchen it didn't immediately register what exactly was wrong with Billie and Kester, slumped sideways in their chairs, with those bags over their heads. Some sort of game, I thought. Then I saw Sophie's little feet sticking out of a garbage bag on the counter.

At the same moment Orson resumed his barking outside. When he finally stopped, I heard another sound. Under the table, which still had one untouched saucer of pills on it, Carlos was retching inside his plastic bag.

Bas hasn't just brought seeds; he has also brought me a tray of lobelia and a pale pink water lily for the pond. He carries the stuff into the garden, via the back gate, the same way he would enter in the days when, shoulder to shoulder, we battled the wild honeysuckle and other foes.

Hesitantly I get up from my chair on the terrace, where I've been waiting for him all afternoon. Now that he's here, I suddenly feel as attractive as a hippo. Come on, Billie, help me out a little.

"Well," he says frankly, "for someone who's been away this long, you certainly look pale."

"Hello to you too," I reply.

His eyes shift to the ice bucket in which I'm chilling a bottle of white wine. One little glass won't do Ida-Sophie any harm.

"So here we are then," he says awkwardly when I've poured him a glass.

"You can say that again." Is it the fact that I've lied to him that's come between us? It is now safe to confess that I've never been away. It wouldn't be putting Lucia in any danger at this point.

"Lovely weather, isn't it?" he says, fidgeting on his chair.

"Yes. Cheers."

"To your health. How's it all going, by the way, with . . ." He waves at my stomach.

"Oh, fine, couldn't be better," I say automatically. Oh damn, now I've blown my chance.

We both look at the conifers that survived our pruning frenzy. A couple of the cypresses have turned brown.

I start, lamely, "The lobelia might do well over there . . ."

"Did you ever get my card?"

"Yes, now that you mention it, I did."

He grimaces nervously. "Point is, from the moment you showed up here again, something's been bugging me. Or even longer, actually. I really need to talk to you about it."

"What do you mean?"

"I meant to tell you right away, but I was afraid of opening up old wounds, so I was hoping you'd bring up the subject yourself of . . . you know, what happened, then." He looks at me askance. *Then.* A carefully selected word.

It makes my blood run cold. What's he after, some sort of sick thrill, just like Marlies and Gerda and all the others? What does he want from me? What does he want me to tell him? Why I didn't run straight to my parents in the sunroom, for instance? Because isn't that how a totally panic-stricken twelve-year-old would normally have reacted? What instinct compelled me to haul Carlos from under the table and drag him hastily down to the cellar? He was gagging and his lips were blue.

Bas leans toward me. "I've got to show you this, Ellen. I must." He holds out a piece of paper, folded twice.

I open it. It's one of my father's old memos. His clear handwriting, the wide spacing, the ornate capital letters. Involuntarily I clench my eyes shut. Then I open them again, wide.

"Note the date." He points.

6 April 1973.

Early in the morning of April 7, the police, alerted by Bas, the first to arrive at the office as always, had discovered the five dead bodies in the house. There had been no sign of violence or forced entry.

Uncomprehendingly I stare at the grubby memo in my hand: on the day prior to that fateful evening, my father, in this memo, had asked Bas to book a trip for two to Florida. He stressed that it was to be a surprise for my mother. A second honeymoon.

Bas put his hand on my arm. "Do you understand, Ellen? This isn't a request from someone who is intending to . . . I showed it to the police, at the time. They agreed it was certainly strange, but then, well, there was also that note from your parents . . ."

"That one sentence, you mean. Which didn't explain a thing."

"Right. The one that said they'd seen to it that you would not suffer. Wasn't that it? So the investigation ended up concluding that your parents themselves had — that they consciously and deliberately . . ." He is beginning to sweat. He glares at me fiercely. "Your parents were such kind, decent people! I'm sure there must have been some maniac involved. A murderer, who forced them to write that . . . Don't you work in a forensic lab? Couldn't there be some other evidence that may have been overlooked? After all this time, it's probably too late to prove anything, of course, but isn't it possible, in theory, that the police made a mistake? I've never been able to shake that conviction. And then, when you suddenly reappeared on the scene, I knew I had to show you your father's note. He didn't intend . . . he can never have intended . . . Here it is, in his own words, in black and white! And I never could believe it of your mother, either. They were proud of all of you! They loved you! They didn't have any reason not to want to see you grow up! Do you know what your father used to say about you? That you were his —"

"Stop it!" I shriek. I am in such a state that I have to hold on to the edge of the table.

"But . . . I only wanted to cheer you up. I thought you . . ." His face, slick with perspiration, quivers.

Twenty-five years he's been thinking

about us, not that anyone ever asked him to. He has been tossing and turning in his bed, convinced that my parents loved their children. While in reality they only had eyes for each other. We were the mere by-products of their love: its proof in the flesh, as it were. Of course there would never have been a tragedy if my mother's hormones hadn't gone haywire, but when the crucial moment came, my father chose her, not us. He let himself be dragged along, instead of holding her back. A suicide pact: the ultimate, perverted, romantic ideal. While Kester, Billie, and Sophie were breathing their last, he was lying with his head in her lap, besotted. There can be no forgiveness for that, ever. You have to harden your heart, for always.

There is nothing in the world more monstrous than what my father did. With his eyes wide open, he consented to the death of his own children. And it's the very enormity of what he did that pushes Bas even now to clutch foolishly at straws. Anything rather than face the truth: the awful truth that people can, indeed, be monsters.

He says, "Oh, Ellen, oh please, forgive me. I just wanted to offer you another perspective . . ." He is squirming on his chair.

I want to scream in his face that the pills

intended to knock us out were dished out right before my very eyes. Didn't they tell you that at the police station, Bas, that I gave them a statement to that effect, stammering through my tears? Is that useful to you, Bas? How does that jibe with your theories?

I'd been stupid enough to think of Bas as my silent, knowing witness. I thought he was the only one in the whole world who didn't need to be fed chapter and verse in order to make sense of it all.

"Just get out of here, for God's sake!" I bellow. "And don't you even think of reminding me that I told you to buzz off before. This is different. You'll never set foot here again."

He gets up, speechless.

After a pause, he finally says, "You can always give me a ring."

"Fat chance," says Billie laconically.

Once, long ago, there was a party at the Unicorn. It was the night of the summer solstice. We all guzzled beer under the tall trees, with Sjaak turning a blind eye. Someone talked about Stonehenge. Someone else was beating on a Celtic drum.

The air smelled of primeval things and the grass our therapeutic counselors were smoking.

Since I had no one to talk to, I beheld the proceedings from the sidelines, sitting by myself on an empty beer crate. At some point, a toddler came waddling by, pants sagging, a bright bandanna knotted around his dirty hair. Thinking he was new, I asked him, out of pure boredom, which pavilion he lived in. He lisped, surprised and indignant: "With Dada," pointing to Sjaak.

I had never considered where Sjaak might be off to after sitting down to dinner with us every night. So there you had it: all this time, Sjaak of the faded red 2CV and the Palestinian scarf, Sjaak of the Van Nelle tobacco breath and the tarnished Indian rings, had secretly been leading a whole self-contained second life on the side. So we weren't enough for him. He just had to have himself a grubby little brat as well.

I gave his son a spiteful shove, sending him sprawling on the grass. He started bawling.

Sjaak heard him immediately, over the pounding of the drum. His head swiveled in the little boy's direction as if the two of them were tied together by an invisible thread. He jumped up and advanced on us with long, weaving strides. He was already quite stoned. "What's up, Frodo?" he asked. "Come on, man, we're supposed to be having a good time."

"She pushed me," the little boy sniveled, scrambling to his feet and rubbing his eyes with both his fists.

Sjaak trained a hazy stare on me.

"I'm not your baby-sitter," I snarled. "I suppose you expect me to keep an eye on him while you're sitting there smoking your brains out!"

"You know that's not necessary, Ellen. Cool it, will you?" He laid his hand on Frodo's head.

The two of them looked as alike as Billie had looked like my mother, as I had looked like my . . . I couldn't contain myself. "I want a father too!" I wailed.

"Well, not much we can do about that, can we? It sucks, though, doesn't it, kid?"

Having let my despair out, I couldn't keep a lid on it anymore. "Can't I come and live with you?"

He frowned, pensive and considering. "No can do, kid; we have another little one on the way as it is, and we've just got this little flat in Schalkwijk. We don't have a spare room for you."

"But I've never had a room of my own! I couldn't care less! I'll sleep on the sofa!" I was breathing so hard that it was making me dizzy. "I'll dry the dishes every night! Promise! And I'll change the baby's diaper, I'm the best diaper-changer ever!"

He shook his head, taking a nervous drag on his joint.

I was going all black and blue inside. Helplessly, I whimpered, "How come nobody wants me?"

"They don't want adolescents. Look at Marlies and Gerda. Nothing wrong with them, great kids, but you can't get anybody to take them, not for all the tea in China. That's life, my girl. It's got nothing to do with you. You're just going to have to stick it out here until you turn eighteen."

Eighteen! I might be dead by then. "Asshole!" I yelled.

"Hey, swearing isn't going to make it better," said Sjaak, pulling his headband a little lower over his forehead. He hesitated and seemed to be making up his mind about something. "But I've got something for you anyway. A present. Come." He took my hand.

"Me too!" cried Frodo, and with a start I suddenly thought of Carlos, who was now Michael Kamphuis, and I felt I couldn't go on, I really couldn't go on.

"Hey, King Kong, why don't you go climb that tree over there," said Sjaak. "And when I get back, I expect you to be sitting up there, do you hear me? And then you can jump down, and I'll catch you."

We walked side by side to our pavilion, past the campfires with smoke curling up into the still night air, past softly singing and swaying people who were holding onto each other tight, so tight it made you grit your teeth.

He said, "Marti and I have been saving it specially for you. She said I could give it to you when I thought it was the right time. Since your memory has been in such excellent working order again lately, I think the time has come."

To be honest, I never could understand why they always made such a fuss over my memory. Those first few weeks at the Unicorn were the ones I'd enjoyed the most, when I'd thought it was a summer camp and I'd impressed everyone with my stories about the lovely Helen of Troy. Was this present something I really wanted?

"You'll love it," he promised, taking a flat bundle out of the dresser in the living room. It was wrapped in brown paper.

It was our old photo album, with the

padded cover and the spiderweb tissue paper between the pages. My mother always pasted in the pictures; my father wrote the captions. "Michael and his Lego castle," and then the date.

That I was disappointed is putting it mildly. I really flipped my lid this time; they had to lock me up in a dark little room with just a mattress in it. They let me out three days later.

That odious, insulting photo album! All those meaningless shots of normal-looking adults and children going about their perfectly ordinary business. There was nothing that foreshadowed the doom that awaited us. A boy on a bicycle. A girl emptying a bag of groceries. A mother and a bowl of apples. A father with a baby on his lap. There was simply no connection between what I could see in those snapshots and what happened to us next. It might as well have been the photo album of a family of total strangers.

That's why I packed it away.

Most of the time I forgot I even had it.

Years later, when moving from place to place, from one room to the next, I'd sometimes find myself weighing it in my hands, wondering why I'd ever bothered keeping it. I never even showed it to Thijs. It's only since Ida-Sophie has started asking to see it that it has become a regular fixture in our lives.

And then something else occurs to me. I never thought of it before, but haven't those old snapshots begun to mean something again since I started looking at them through Ida-Sophie's eyes, as it were?

I carry the wine bucket and glasses into the kitchen. I empty the bottle I had intended to share with Bas down the drain. It's important to keep a clear head now.

I find the album in the sunroom. I carry it out to the terrace. Here it is, the one of my mother with the apples. That picture didn't mean much to me before. Now I can spin a whole story around it for Sophie-Ida. Where do these stories come from? Have I pieced them together accurately from events that happened, things I must have been subconsciously aware of at the time, fleshed out by what I now know of my mother's condition? Or, in order to make sense of it all, have I been attributing actions, thoughts, and motives to my parents that I've simply made up?

Still, making stuff up is hard work. Your imagination can easily falter, while these stories well up in me fully formed, fluent and unhesitating. Is it because Ida-Sophie is prompting me? Am I the storyteller, or is she?

I tap my belly gently. Of course. It is you. You know infinitely more than I do: you're the one who was always around, without a break, while I was at school or playing in the garden with my dog. Mama never let you out of her sight for a second. You even slept at the foot of the conjugal bed. You heard my parents talking in the intimacy of their bedroom. So then tell me. Why didn't my father stop her? What made him do it?

Finally I shall have the answer.

I turn the pages in a frenzy. There aren't that many photos of him. He was usually the photographer. All right, here! Right after your birth, when you were such a screamer. You're lying on his lap, howling. He's gazing at you with infinite concern. He feels his heart constrict. He's thinking, If you'd known beforehand how deeply your children's pains and sorrows would touch you, you would never have started a family. But what's done is done, and so you're left with just one desire, primitive and futile: you want them all to be well and happy.

I quickly leaf through the rest, in search of a later picture of him. But here we are at the last page already. There's Carlos with his Lego castle. Right behind him, my mother with her radiant smile. She's saying: "It's quite magnificent. So are you going to make some knights for it next?"

Carlos nods.

"And horses too?"

"One horse. For sharing."

"Most practical. While you do that I'll go and put the clothes in the washing machine."

In the bathroom she sorts the dirty laundry by color. Now that everything is decided, even the most menial task makes her happy. For every day could be her last, and she is thankful for every moment that's left for her to smell Kester's socks or mop up the mud left by Ellen's shoes. When your final hour is near, it is the most trivial everyday things that give the most pleasure, that are the most significant: for this is the raw material of your happy family life and must be savored to the last drop.

Long has she lived in fear and darkness, but all that is now past. Serenely she switches on the washing machine and then goes to take a peek in at Ida, to see if she's still asleep. She bends over the crib and kisses her softly on the tip of her nose.

She had to hurt her little girl because God demanded it. For months she did all she could to drive the sin from that frail little body, and to render the whole of Ida's environment pure. But that wasn't good enough for God. No sacrifice, no matter how terrible, was sufficient for Him. He knew no mercy. So what else could she do, in her despair, but punish Him for His remoteness by assuming His place on His throne herself? Merciful God, indeed! Merciful Mama, that was the truth. She explained this to Ida in a whisper, while jamming a potato-peeler up her vagina.

After that, the darkness had grown impenetrable. For who was there to address her breathless supplications to now? And, come to think of it, who was there to keep the universe spinning, who was there to arrange the stars in the night sky? It was all up to her now, and if she hadn't adored Ida so, so much that she'd willingly lay down her own life for her baby's, she'd have given up long ago from exhaustion.

She dressed her daughter's wounds and then gave her new ones, swamped by her responsibilities. While preparing a meal, while helping Sybille with her homework or applying Michael's ointment, she also had to produce floods on the other side of the world, drowning whole villages in mud; she caused volcanoes to spew hot lava, she caused children in desolate wastelands to starve to death, corrupt colonels to stage coups, the orangutan to be driven to near extinction; she saw to it that in every alley in the world people were raped, mugged, and kicked to death, that a space rocket at Cape Kennedy exploded on the launchpad, that leprosy broke out in Calcutta, and that a heartbroken Elvis Presley slowly ate himself to death in Graceland.

The baby whimpered, her poor little body twitching all over. How they suffered together. When was this ghastly torment going to end? Why should the two of them be responsible for all the wickedness in the world? Why had evil, in all its cunning, chosen her innocent family as its breeding ground? Daily it made its presence felt in her loved ones. In the sudden lewdness of her sweet Sybille's glances, in the uncontrollably swelling breasts that Ellen was helplessly struggling with, in Frits's bestial assault, he who had always been respect and tenderness itself — only little Michael and Kester remained unsullied, but for how much longer?

"We must protect them," she told Ida. "While their souls are still pure, we must save them." Agitated, she paced back and forth with the baby in her arms. Her fine young sons, multitalented Kester, Michael with his — but little Michael had already been marked! Her knees turned to jelly at the thought: Michael's scalding had been the first omen of what was in store for the whole family.

Now her panic knew no bounds. She knelt with Ida on the sharp pebbles of the garden path and tried calling on God to come back. She pleaded, *Take me, but please don't hurt my children.* She lay prostrate, paralyzed at the thought that God and evil must be one and the same. And that she, by taking His place, had become an accomplice: she was the Third Entity in an Unholy Trinity, sowing destruction, groping around with ever-lengthening tentacles.

She would have to smite water from a stone.

She would have to ignite a burning bush.

She would have to issue Laws: honor the devil and all his creatures, or thou shalt burn in hell for all eternity.

The trick was to try to outfox the Evil One himself. Humbly she told him that he could have her share of world domination; she would step down voluntarily. That is, if, in return, he agreed not to claim the souls of her children and husband for his hellfire.

Ha! he jeered.

She would not let it go. She was his handmaiden; she was entitled to certain privileges. Or at least he owed her blood money: her rightful wages. Coolly and eloquently she demanded that which was due to her. She wanted amnesty for her family, that was all: the only thing she asked was that her children and her husband be spared from eternal hellfire and its unspeakable torments. She fought like a tigress for her brood. But the devil wouldn't even grant her the courtesy of a reply.

She was crushed to her very marrow. Not even the devil would negotiate with her. So then, what difference did it make — day or night, life or death? She gave up. She was exhausted — besides, what else was there left for her to do?

She laid Ida down in her crib and caressed the ravaged little body. All had been in vain.

It would be Easter soon. She'd make some little Easter chicks and, for Michael, a funny Easter bunny. She had started rummaging mechanically through drawers and cupboards for the raw materials — the wire, the red card for the beaks — when the irony of it suddenly struck her: now that all hope was gone, irrevocably and forever, here she was getting things ready for the day of hope, the feast of the Resurrection.

Bewildered, she sat down at the kitchen table where a year ago, after the Easter egg hunt, they had informed the children of Ida's forthcoming arrival. Like every ardently wanted child, Ida had been a child of hope. But didn't the fact that it was Easter mean that she was also the child of the Resurrection?

Everything finally began to fall into place. Ida had been sent to this family with a mission. The same mission as that of the innocent babe who had been born in a manger two thousand years ago — that is, to remind the world of the existence of evil, and to fight it as a vulnerable mortal. Her little daughter's suffering made perfect sense now. All that remained to make her immortal was — death. She would shrug the gravestone aside and ascend to heaven, chaste and pure forever; the redeemed and the redeemer. Exalted above every Law, unassailable, sovereign. Supreme.

"But is death what I gave birth to you for, then?" she asked aloud, still only half able to grasp her mission, just like that woman in Galilee.

She closed her eyes. Life eternal for her tormented child. Slowly shock gave way to gratitude and resignation.

It was quiet in the house. In the office they were hard at work; the children were still at school. She got up and touched one of the walls in wonder. Here, in this house, the miracle had taken place unheeded; here Ida had been born. The moon had been nearly full, it had been a cold night, but apart from that it had seemed a night like any other. Why did such things only ever reveal themselves in hindsight?

She hiked up her skirt and touched herself. Her vulva was throbbing and burning. Out of this blistering heat and out of these loins Ida was born. It was for this that she herself had been destined her whole life, innocent as she had been. It had been preordained even when, as a child, her sour parents had drummed into her over and over again, "Just remember you're nothing special."

This was why she had married Frits van Bemmel.

Their entire marriage had been nothing

but the groundwork leading up to this very moment. She sank to her knees beside the crib. The baby's eyes, glazed and dulled from crying, stared at her blankly.

Margje bowed her head. "Thy will be done," she whispered to Ida. "Deliver us from evil, forever and ever, amen."

Such a load fell from her shoulders then, it felt as if her heart would float up into the sky. Without further deliberation she picked up Ida in her arms. Carrying her over to the drainboard, she brushed aside the breadcrumbs and laid Ida down on her back on the granite. Choosing a butcher's knife from the knife block, she began whetting it with long, powerful strokes. She felt a charge of strength and self-assurance surging through her. She was one of the chosen. She was the instrument of Ida's will.

The knife gleamed dully. She ran the blade between her fingers. Then she raised it up high, pulling Ida's shirt up to her chin with her other hand.

It would be an Easter celebration like no other. Behind her, on the kitchen table, lay the materials to make the Easter chicks and the bunny. And there were the eggs to be painted too, the children and she would do that together this evening.

Suddenly she caught sight of herself reflected in the windowpane, poised with the knife in her hand. Gasping for breath, she covered her face with her hands, overcome with horror. The knife clattered to the ground. Dazed, she collapsed into a chair. She couldn't keep her teeth from chattering.

What had made her think Ida's death would be enough? Did she have any sort of guarantee that her death would suffice to ward off the Evil One? The devil himself had planted this heinous idea in her head. Satan was trying to trick her into taking some bogus half-measure in order to keep the rest of her family in his clutches. She began to sob desperately. Only when Frits and the rest of the children were dead, wrapped in the sanctity of martyrdom, would they be saved from the fires of hell.

At first she balked, thinking, But I'll never see Michael lose his baby teeth. Kester has been saving up for a motorbike for nothing. Sybille will never marry; Ellen won't go to the university. Then her defiance evaporated, because weren't those mere trifles in the larger scheme of things? Wasn't it just her selfish mother's heart talking here? Love — what a horrendously possessive thing that was. For what was the sacrifice of their life on earth anyway, compared with the dazzling glory of the hereafter?

If she hesitated now, they would remain the devil's helpless playthings forever and ever. She had to make up her mind now, in this very moment of revelation. She wanted to beg, "But at least let me keep Frits." Let me have someone to comfort me, in all the coming days of loneliness and all the nights of darkness. Don't leave me here alone.

But would he be able to stomach living under the same roof as her? He would never understand; he would curse her; he would despise her; he would immediately turn against her. Even now, when her sacrifice was still only an intention, he would loathe her for it if he knew. He would raise his hand against her. In his ignorance, he would do everything in his power to stop her. Without his children, his life would not be worth living. She would lose his love forever.

She rushed over to Ida, who was feebly kicking one of her legs, her shirt still hiked up over her chest. Margje took the little foot in her hand. Those toes so like Frits's. If she wanted to keep their love alive, the love she had never doubted, in spite of the

324

devil who had come between them, then Frits and she would have to join their children in death.

Ida was breathing uneasily. She was trying to squirm out of her mother's grip. Her little hands knotted into fists.

"Then give me the strength to do it, dammit!" Margje screamed at her.

Somewhere overhead a door slammed. She looked up, startled. Then it was quiet again. She thought of her husband sitting at his desk, of her children on their way home from school. Right! Time to make a decision!

Then Ida opened her mouth. She shrieked at the top of her lungs, little arms flailing. And, one by one, Margje deciphered the words falling from her chalky lips: "We'll — see to it — that — they don't — suffer —"

That clinched it.

Frantically she yanked open a drawer, found a pen and notepad, and wrote down Ida's covenant scrupulously, word for word. That done, already more sure of herself, she tore off the top sheet and burned the rest of the notepad. She sprinkled the ashes over her own head and that of the baby.

Until such time as the devil decided to

give it another try, she was now finally entitled to some rest. Living on borrowed time, she would use the respite to enjoy her family again to the fullest. She did not need to combat evil anymore. She had already overcome it, with Ida's help.

With one last lingering glance at my mother's happy face, I snap the album shut. The garden is deadly still. Dusk is drawing in. The birds are quiet, and there isn't a breath of wind to make the trees rustle. Slowly I get up and amble inside. My footsteps echo down the empty hall. I stop at the cellar door. This is the only place in the house that I have deliberately avoided until now. But this is the place where I have to be, if I am ever to pick up the thread again: this is the place where that thread snapped twenty-five years ago.

It takes some doing to open the door. The lock is rusty, the wood warped. Billie's old refuge has obviously not been used in years.

Cautiously I descend the creaky stairs and then lower myself, awkwardly because of my fat stomach, onto one of the bottom steps. I inhale the musty air and look around.

Billie's platform of planks is still there, all rotten and slimy with mold. I can make out a couple of candles stuck onto saucers, and dishes with decomposing incense. You can still read *Kilroy was here* in faint letters on the damp wall. Hardly a thing has been touched since the night I hid here with Carlos, in mortal terror.

I think of my father, but I have no tears — neither tears of relief because I finally understand what really happened, nor tears of pity because he too was just a victim, nor tears of regret over the bitter hatred I unjustly felt for him all this time.

I hug my stomach in my arms and rock Ida-Sophie, the way I rocked Carlos down here twenty-five years ago. I just couldn't wake him up, no matter how hard I pinched him. In my panic I shook him so violently that he threw up.

Was my father already dead at that point? Had he been dead when I had seen him stretched out in the sunroom, or had he only been knocked out by the sleeping pills and Valium my mother had been squirreling away? Had he been dreaming peacefully about the trip to Florida he was about to surprise her with, now that she was her old self again? A dazzling white beach fringed with palm trees, a flight of pink flamingos, cocktails in tall frosted glasses.

From somewhere very far away, Orson's

barking must have bored its way into his brain when I returned home with my dog. Oh, there's Ellen, he must have thought woozily; she still has to take her vitamins, or else Margje will have a fit. He tried to shake off his drowsiness in order to urge me to get on with it, but his body refused to comply. Trying to struggle out of his drugged state in vain, like a drowning man trying to reach the surface, he must have realized that there was something fishy about the pills my mother had distributed. Perhaps the thought had even flashed through his mind, I must warn Ellen.

"I'm sorry, Dad," I say out loud. "I didn't know. I really had no idea."

Now the tears do come. Every tear scorches me with shame and regret, like the ashes raining down on Pompeii, which I had once excitedly told him about after a history lesson. He had listened attentively, as always, his feet resting on the bottom drawer of his desk. "Even the bread on people's tables and the dogs sleeping underneath were turned to stone! Isn't that amazing, Dad?"

That night I'd had a nightmare in which I was drowning in boiling lava; I woke up the whole house with my terrified screams. My father had come to sit by me in his pajamas. He massaged my shoulders until they relaxed. "That can't happen here, darling, you're safe here," he soothed me.

I gulped down a few last sobs, only half believing him. Live cinders could come hurtling through the roof at any minute.

"Besides, look what I have for you!"

I looked. I couldn't see a thing. But then he waved his hand like a magician. And even though his hands were still empty, I now could clearly see that he was snapping open an umbrella and holding it over my head. I let out a sigh of wonder.

"Here, take it. Hold on to it tight," he said, offering me his fist. Then he kissed me good night.

Huddled on the cellar stairs, I wipe the tears from my eyes. Deep inside my chest, in the place where it's always been dank and chilled because for three-quarters of my life my heart has been a thing of stone, like the bread of Pompeii and its dogs, I suddenly feel a warm glow. All the old hatred and fury have been crushed to rubble and crumble away.

Under Daddy's umbrella, he'd told me, nothing bad will ever happen to you, Ellen. Never.

Maybe — just maybe — I owed my survival to the potency of his vow, to the magic mantle of his protection. For a parent's promise of safety, given to a frightened child, must surely be the most important promise that is ever made in this life. It's a pledge of such phenomenal power that even fate must yield to it.

I press my hand to my chest and feel my heartbeat, the heart that is finally able to say, Daddy, you were fine just the way you were. I was wrong about him, but then I was just a child. And I was also wrong about myself. I am not who I thought I was: the abandoned daughter of a weakling. In order to make it up to him and to his memory, I shall have to accomplish a full revision of my self, layer upon layer. "I'll do it," I mutter. "Yes I will." Then I look up.

Billie and Kester are standing in front of me, holding hands.

"What's up?" I whisper.

"You know very well what's up," says Kester, just as softly.

"It's curtains for us, then," says Billie. She smiles uncertainly.

I hoist myself to my feet in alarm, seeking support from the mottled wall.

Kester comes closer, dragging his feet. "You're not just going to give us up like this, are you?"

Billie stammers, "We really don't deserve this, Ellen. Without us you'd have long . . ."

"I'd long have what?" I blurt out. "Without you I'd have had pals and girlfriends, without you my marriage wouldn't have . . ." I am shocked by the truth of my own words.

"That's so mean!" says Billie. "Without us you would never have known love. You've said so yourself at least a thousand times!"

I am silent. The thing that I used to call love — was that really the right word for it? I'm not what you could call an expert in the field. I look at their pale, translucent faces. I take a deep breath. One thing's for sure. As long as I refuse to let go of them, part of me will always remain the twelve-year-old I once was. The frightened, confused child.

"I have to get on with my life," I say in a stifled voice.

Kester combs his fingers through his hair. Then he digs his hands into his pockets. "Loyalty, Ellen, is a virtue."

Those were my father's words, the time Billie bolted at the Scallop Ford. He also taught me that time that to be loyal, you have to know how to choose. You have to be very careful which way you choose. Besides, there is such a thing as being loyal to yourself, too.

"You'll never be able to get us back, never, Ellen, if you push us out now," Billie cautions me sadly. "You'll lose us forever."

"No," I say, with calm certainty, "that's not true, because I won't live forever. I will come back to you one day." I am smiling through my tears. "It's only temporary. It's only for the rest of my life."

I pause at the top of the cellar stairs. I reach for the door handle. I suddenly feel sick. What if I'm locked in here! Dazed, I shake my head. No, that was then; this is now.

I can fling the door wide open if I want to, but I don't. I think of my father and re-alize I'll always be a slave to phantoms until I finally face it — what it was like, that night, to be huddled down here with Carlos. I have never allowed myself to dwell on it before. That night has always remained a gaping hole in my memory.

For a second I hesitate. Then I lumber down the stairs again. In the darkest, far-thest corner, I sink down on the ground, propping myself up, arms at my sides, on the wooden planks. It was here. This is where we sat.

I was so scared that I almost longed for my parents to find us. I couldn't believe how naughty I was being. I'd be sent to death row for refusing to swallow my vitamin pills and hiding down here with my little brother who just wouldn't wake up. He felt limp and clammy in my arms. He stank of vomit. His breathing was rapid and shallow.

The house creaked all around me.

Condensation trickled down the cellar walls, as if the walls were weeping.

The sound of the blood hammering in my ears was so loud that I couldn't hear whether my parents were looking for me, calling out my name. I rolled Carlos off my lap and laid him on his side on the ground. My legs almost refused to carry me as I scrambled up the stairs. I felt for the key I had turned on the inside of the door. But I couldn't get it to budge, no matter how hard I jiggled it. My hands grew clammy. "Mama!" I screamed. "Daddy!"

Upstairs Billie and Kester were probably snickering at *The Monkees* on television, and Sophie was being fed a mashed banana before being put to bed. It must have been a prank, those plastic bags. How could I have thought anything different, even for a moment? Weeping with self-reproach, I sat huddled against the door.

Why weren't they looking for me? I listened hard but couldn't hear a sound. It must be late. They wouldn't all have just gone to bed, would they? Were they punishing me by making me stay in the cellar all night, was that it? Had Dad and Mama decided that I . . .

Suddenly I get it. It finally hits me, like a thunderbolt. "She simply forgot me," I say out loud, astounded. "She just had too much on her mind."

After all, in her final hour my mother had had to do everything by herself. She must have been rushing feverishly back and forth between the sunroom and the kitchen, hurry, hurry, quite beside herself, the bags, the elastic bands, how do you kill a whole family in one fell swoop, first Billie and Kester, as soon as they started nodding off at the kitchen table, Carlos and Sophie next, a kitchen full of dead children, the terrible euphoria at the thought that her task was almost done, now only Frits left, and herself.

And all that time, I was out on the beach, laughing, throwing sticks for my dog, a delirious Orson and I running after seagulls that screeched indignantly at being disturbed. Black and dangerous as any hellhound, he loped wildly along the shoreline. The tide was out; seashells crunched under my feet; once or twice I half slipped on a washed-up jellyfish.

When I couldn't see a thing in the dark anymore except for the white frothy rims of the waves, I realized it must be much later than I'd thought. I raced home on my bicycle as fast as I could.

I can still remember how raw the wet night air felt, how on the bicycle path I couldn't hear any sound except the whirring of the headlight on my front wheel. I remember I was planning to surprise everyone with a cup of hot chocolate when I got home, with frothed milk. Then I would help Carlos into his pajamas and read him a story, as I did every night. My parents would come and kiss him good night when I was done, and my father would pinch my cheek, a pinch that said, "You are the cement, Ellen. Where would we be without you?"

People say that the truth is always better than gnawing doubt. Is it really so? It is true that for twenty-five years I have woken up every morning wondering why I had to be the one to survive the tragedy. But the answer is just too disturbing.

Because I had gone out that evening, I had simply been overlooked.

In her panic and agitation, my mother never missed me. The fact of my existence simply slipped her mind. If she had had the chance to pause for just one moment, just long enough to think, *Ellen!*, then I might have felt it, two miles away, on the deserted beach; I might even have heard her.

But my mother had forgotten me.

# *Epilogue*

Chattering thrushes are squabbling over the first berries in the yew and holly. The hawthorn bushes lining the garden path flaunt their crimson leaves; toadstools sprout in every humid hollow. You get this urge to start chopping wood and making pumpkin soup.

Everyone agrees that it's an unforgettably lovely autumn. It's the middle of October, and you can still often sit outside.

The real estate agent has been around three times with hopeful buyers: someone from an advertising agency, someone else from a law office, a third in search of a home for the day care center she is starting. I don't care who buys it. I'm not involved in the house tours, the negotiations, the offers and counteroffers. I'm almost too heavy now to climb the stairs, and my thoughts are preoccupied with the imminent labor and delivery.

When I receive a phone call informing me that the deed is done and Bureau Van Bemmel will be reincarnated as an advertising agency, I have a fleeting moment of regret about the garden, which I shall have to give up. "Can you move out in three months' time?" asks the real estate man.

That means we'll be here through Christmas, with plenty of time to find ourselves a new home. It couldn't be better. I'm so elated that I phone Bas at work and ask him to dinner. Sauerkraut and sausages, I propose. Bas is a man of simple but robust tastes.

That same evening, he busies himself setting the table while I jab at juniper berries with a fork. My protruding belly collides with the stove, and immediately little elbows give a prod of protest, little knees wrestle, little feet kick. It's all go in there. She certainly is fired up. She can hardly wait any longer.

"Penny for your thoughts," says Bas. He takes the fork out of my hand and looks at me searchingly. He isn't a saint, by any means: if I rub him the wrong way too often, I'll lose him. We are just two people cautiously trying to make it work, like everyone else.

"I still can't decide," I reply. "I've got a list here, it's as long as my arm, but I can't make up my mind."

"Here, show me that list," he says, turning down the flame under the potatoes. He still knows how to do only one thing at a time. I find it endearing.

I hand over the sheet of paper. "Why don't you decide," I say. "You decide on the name we'll give her."

# About the Author

Renate Dorrestein is one of Holland's best-loved and best-selling novelists. Born in Amsterdam in 1954, she became a journalist before writing her first novel, *Outsiders*, which was published in 1983. Her books have regularly appeared at the top of the Dutch best-seller lists since then. She has been nominated for the Libris Prize and won the Annie Romein Prize in 1993 for her "original and irresistible" body of work. In 1997 she was voted runner-up for the Publieksprijs for the most popular Dutch writer. *A Heart of Stone* is her first novel to be translated into English.

The employees of Thorndike Press hope you have enjoyed this Large Print book. All our Large Print titles are designed for easy reading, and all our books are made to last. Other Thorndike Press Large Print books are available at your library, through selected bookstores, or directly from us.

For information about titles, please call:

(800) 223-1244
(800) 223-6121

To share your comments, please write:

Publisher
Thorndike Press
P.O. Box 159
Thorndike, Maine 04986